Grainne

For Sarah
(You finally got your wish to have a book in the Aoife O'Reilly series dedicated to you)

Table of Contents

Chapter One

Dublin
1946

"Grainne, no."

She paused on the stairs and turned at her mother's suddenly sharp tone.

Her mother's whole body had become stiff, frozen on the staircase like a statue. Grainne had a mind to ignore her and bound down the stairs into her father's arms like she did every day when he returned home from work, but her mother, somehow always knowing what she was thinking, grabbed her by the arm and pulled her aside. The two of them stood there on the landing, out of sight for half a second, her mother's long, manicured nails digging into the soft flesh of her upper arm. She was about to cry out for her father when *they* showed up. She suddenly understood now why her mother had stopped her, why she'd pulled her out of sight so violently.

Grainne tugged her arm free from her mother's grasp and silently moved to the railing. She peeked over the edge to the foyer below, her stomach swimming with vertigo but she did not look away. Her father came through the front door as usual, but she could tell even from this height that his body was tense, the lines around his eyes harsher, not crinkled and jovial like when he saw her at the end of a long day's work. Following swiftly on his heels was *her*, the woman of the house.

She was a stern woman with an icy cold stare that would cut through you to the bone faster than any winter's wind. Behind her were her children – two boys. Grainne did not like them one bit. She hated that they teased and taunted her, calling her names like "bastard," then laughed cruelly when she started to cry. They were mean and vain, and she hated them ferociously.

Why did they have to show up now? It wasn't their time. They only came here for a short visit during the summer and then were not seen again until the following year. Appearing like this in February was out of character for them.

Even though they were technically the true owners of the house Grainne called her home, she always felt that *they* were the intruders, not her and her mother who lived here all year with her father. She hated the way they would breeze in like an ill wind, causing her father to be tense and stern, his normally happy face always unsmiling in their presence. Most of all, she hated being confined to the servants' quarters, forbidden to enter any of the main rooms lest she and her mother be seen by the lady of the house. Her only reprieve during these interminable visits was if she could sneak down the back stairs out towards the rose garden where the head gardener might let her play for a bit.

"Just make sure an' stay out o' sight," he would whisper to her, and give her a conspiratorial wink.

She would put her index finger to her lips and make a shushing noise, letting him know this was their little secret.

Grainne wondered how long they would be here this time, how long she would be shuttered away for.

"Gracie?" her father called out for her, using her English name. She made a move to head down the stairs towards him, but once again, her mother held her back.

"Gracie?"

"Let me go!" she hissed at her mother, but she did not relent.

"Where is Grace? Bring her here to me now," she heard her father order one of the servants who had come to take his coat.

"No."

There was a long pause, a silent battle of wills being played out between husband and wife, but Grainne knew who would win. *She* won every argument when she was here. After what seemed like an age, her father finally relented.

"Come boys," the lady of the house commanded her sons. "Come spend time with your father."

Grainne heard them move away, heading for the drawing room.

"Come," her mother whispered to her, pulling her away from the railing and back up the stairs towards the servants' quarters. Grainne fought her all the way, but a girl of seven is no match to physically overpower her mother.

"It's not fair!" she wailed when she was shut behind the door of her mother's bedroom. She threw herself face first atop the four-poster bed, balling the floral duvet in her hands and kicking her legs in a full-blown tantrum. "This is *our* house. They don't belong here!"

"This is your father's house," her mother corrected her, ignoring her daughter's outburst, as she so often did. "You and I merely live here. It is a privilege, not a right."

Grainne huffed and puffed until she finally realized it wasn't going to change the fact that the lady of the house and her dreadful sons were here to stay for the immediate future. She would just have to wait them out like before. Then she could have her house, and her father, all to herself again.

഻ജ

As it turned out, they seemed to be in no hurry to depart any time soon. In fact, they seemed to have planted themselves firmly in the house, reclaiming it as their own. After two interminably boring days shut up in her mother's room, her father summoned her mother to his study.

"Stay here," her mother warned her sternly, seeing the hopeful look in Grainne's eyes that maybe she would see her father today.

Grainne harumphed at her mother's order and plopped herself back down on the bed. She idly picked at a loose thread on the quilt that was neatly folded at the edge of the bed, listening to the loud *tick!* of the clock on the mantlepiece above the fireplace. The seconds ticked by like hours, and finally, Grainne had had enough waiting. Tiptoeing towards the door, she silently opened it, peeked around the edge to make sure no one was in the corridor, and padded her way down the carpeted staircase and through the house to her father's study.

The large oak door was slightly ajar, a faint warm light emanating from the fireplace. She heard raised voices coming from inside.

"And what would you like me to do?" she heard her father yell at her mother. His tone was angry, frustrated, hurt. She had never heard him sound like that before.

"If I don't turn you and Gracie out, then she'll divorce me, and I'll be left with nothing."

"You'd have us." Her mother's voice was soft, almost a whisper.

"And what good would that do me?"

It was the first time Grainne had witnessed her father being intentionally cruel. His words filled her with an unbearable sadness.

"All of this is paid for by her father. If she divorces me, this all goes away. I love you and Gracie, but I can't lose all of this. This is my career, my reputation we're talking about. I'd be ruined."

She heard the crack of an open hand hitting flesh. If her father's words had shocked her, her mother striking her father was even more so. Her mother had lashed out at her like that before, but never acted that way with her father. It startled her so much that Grainne jumped and had to put a hand over her mouth to prevent herself from making a noise and being noticed.

"*You're* ruined? And what about me?" Her mother's Kerry accent became thicker the angrier she got. "I can never marry now; no man'd take me in with another man's child. And what employer will keep me on once they find out about Grainne? If the Church or the State found out, they'd be like to take her away from me. Is that what you want for your daughter?"

Her parents were silent so long that Grainne dared poke her head around the slight opening of the door to have a look at them. She noticed her mother striding towards her and barely had time to get out of the way before she breezed past, tears streaming down her pretty face. She didn't notice her daughter sitting there, hiding amongst the shadows of the corridor.

She waited a few moments until her mother had gone back up the stairs, knowing that she would soon go looking for her once she realized she was not in her room. She peered into the study and saw her father standing there, looking through the open door at her mother's retreating form, his cheek red from where she had struck him. He stared through her now, as if she were a ghost from his past.

She supposed, in a way, now she was.

ꙮ

Grainne waited until she heard the soft snoring of her nanny before she silently pulled back the covers and swung her feet over the edge of the bed. The floorboards were cool beneath her bare feet as she tiptoed to the door. She was careful to turn the handle slowly so it would not wake either her nanny or the boys. She hated sleeping in the nursery when the boys were here; she never knew if they would try and wake her in the night to terrorize her, threatening to do all kinds of horrible things to her. It was her habit to sneak across the corridor to her mother's room and sleep in her bed whenever they stayed over, searching out some comfort no matter how cold or distant it was. Her mother was moodier whenever they showed up to stay, sullen and prone to bouts of distemper. The littlest, unexpected thing could set her off, but right now, she was more afraid of what the boys might do to her. Silently turning the handle of her mother's bedroom door, she hoped she would be sound asleep tonight so that she could silently slip into the bed and not be noticed until the dawn appeared.

As soon as she closed the door behind her, she heard her mother's muffled sobs and knew she was still awake. Grainne was torn between risking her mother's wrath or risking the potential terror of the nursery.

"Grainne? Is that you?"

Her mother's voice was thick with tears. She sniffed, and Grainne could see her shape shifting into a sitting position on the bed in the gloomy dark of the room. She shuffled across the room to the bed, hiking up the hem of her nightgown and climbed under the covers. She could see in the dim moonlight that her mother's cheeks were damp with tears and she reached up to touch them. Her mother did not flinch away, which surprised her. Grainne knew in that moment that the altercation she had witnessed earlier was going to change her life forever.

After a moment, her mother spoke. "Come now, let's sleep. We have to rise early."

ꙮ

When Grainne woke, it was still before dawn. She had been woken by her mother's movements around the room as she packed things into a small suitcase she had laid out on the foot of the bed.

"Good. You're awake."

Grainne rubbed her eyes sleepily with the back of her hand. "What are you doing, Mama?"

"You need to go across to the nursery and gather your things, Grainne." There was no good morning greeting, no explanation.

"Go on!" her mother hissed at her in a harsh whisper when she had not moved. "And only pack your clothes. Take nothing else."

Grainne shuffled off the bed, padding her way over to the nursery. She was thankful that both boys and the nanny were still asleep. Quietly as she could, she brought out her little suitcase from under the bed and went silently to the dresser, pulling out her favourite dresses. Her mother had not said where they were going or how long they would be away, so Grainne was not sure what she should take with her. She decided on her favourite pink and yellow, and sky-blue silk dresses that her father had bought for her earlier this year. She also put in some stockings and underwear, figuring she would need those no matter where they were going. She was not sure if she would need gloves or not, but she put in a pair, just in case, as well as some of her favourite ribbons for her hair. She also put in two nightgowns in case they would be staying overnight wherever they were going. Even though her mother had said not to bring anything other than her clothes, she lovingly placed her stuffed rabbit in the suitcase too; she hated going anywhere without him, and she was not sure for how long she would be gone. She did not want him to get lonely if she was to be gone a long time.

Wherever it was they were headed, she could not very well go there in just her nightgown, so she silently changed into the dress and stockings her nanny had laid out for her the night before, grabbed her coat, and took her suitcase across the hall to her mother's room. Her mother had dressed and clicked her almost-full suitcase shut.

“Come on,” she ordered, taking the suitcase in one hand and holding the other out to her daughter.

“Where are we going, Mama?” Grainne asked again, but her mother did not respond, only silently marched her down the main stairs, out through the foyer and into the cool, misty Dublin air, not once looking back behind them.

Grainne had not realized it yet, but this would be the last time she would ever lay eyes on her home. She would never return there, nor would she ever see her father again.

Chapter Two

As it turned out, where they went was worse than Grainne could have ever imagined. The Sisters of Our Lady of Charity were devils who would haunt Grainne's dreams for the rest of her long life.

She and her mother first went to the Magdalen Asylum for Penitent Females. Dublin's streets were quiet this time of the morning, bleary-eyed shopkeepers were opening up for the day, casting them curious glances as they walked past. Grainne was tired from their long walk and she really wanted to rest, but her mother had hold of her hand and was marching them perpetually forward.

The asylum was one of the few places women like her mother could go in their situation, which was not saying much for the kind of help offered to women in her mother's position.

"Where are we going?" Grainne asked for what felt like the thousandth time since leaving her father's house. Her mother had never answered her before, so it came as a bit of a surprise when she finally spoke to her.

"The only place we can."

Grainne was not sure she liked the ominous sound of her mother's tone and was beginning to think she had been better off not asking.

"How long will we be staying there?" She was afraid of the answer.

"For as long as we need to."

The two of them continued on in silence for awhile, the only sound was the clicking of her mother's heels upon the paving stones. After a couple of more blocks, they turned down a street lined with brick Georgian terraces from a long-forgotten time. They came upon the asylum and her mother rapped the brass knocker on the front door. They waited patiently until a woman appeared at the door.

"Can I help you?"

"I'm seeking shelter for my daughter and I."

The stern-looking woman gave them a once over, taking in everything about them. Grainne wasn't sure what conclusion she had come to about them, but from the grimace that twisted her mouth, it did not seem to be a favourable one.

"Come inside." The older woman held the door open for them, ushering them into a small office just off the main corridor. She sat herself comfortably behind the desk leaving them to stand before her like the beggars they were, for there were no other chairs in the room. She offered them no greeting, no comfort; she did not even tell them her name.

"And what has brought you here to the asylum?" she asked, bringing up a dark brown ledger and a pen.

"My daughter and I have nowhere to stay," her mother responded carefully. She looked down at the floor and shuffled her feet a bit.

"No husband to provide for you and your daughter? No other family who could take you in?"

"No."

The woman looked like she was going to ask a follow-up question, but decided against it, writing something down in her ledger.

"And you and your daughter were both baptised in the Protestant church?" the stern-looking woman asked.

Grainne did not know why her mother did not lie in that moment, but it would be a decision that would forever define their futures. It was a decision Grainne would come to hate her for.

"No." The woman looked up at her sharply. "I mean, Grainne has been baptised in the church of her father."

The other woman's eyes narrowed as she took in this information. "But you are not."

"No."

Once more she wrote something down in the ledger. She did not speak for a long moment while she wrote, and Grainne felt uneasy. Even at such a young age, she knew that it was important in Ireland to define oneself by one's religion. She knew that her mother's religion set her apart from her daughter. She just had never been confronted with how important this difference between them was until now. Finally, the woman put her pen down.

"The girl can stay here with us," she said. Her unspoken implication was clear: only Grainne would be allowed to stay.

"We stay together." Grainne's mother's voice was firm. She stared at the other woman, her gaze never wavering. "My daughter and I do not get separated. She stays with me."

The woman in charge leaned back in her chair, steepling her fingers as she peered at them over her fingertips.

"In that case, you might try the Sisters of Our Lady of Charity. They may be willing to take you in, but I must ask that you consider your daughter's well-being. The Sisters…let's just say that your daughter might have a better chance of finding a good Protestant home to be fostered in, or even adopted into if she remained here."

Grainne looked up at her mother, startled by this thought. It was unthinkable to her that she would be separated from her mother, let alone that she would be sent to live with another family. Her mother was a hard woman at times, but she was the only mother Grainne had known. She could not conceive of being sent away from her.

"No. My daughter and I stay together. We won't take up any more of your time. Thank you for your help."

Her mother clasped her hand tightly, as if to ward off the other woman from any thoughts of snatching her away. She marched the two of them out of the office and back into the cool morning air, the coolness stinging Grainne's cheeks a bit and marking them with a rosy blush. She followed her mother along the cobblestones, trying to keep up with her brisk pace. She would wish later in life that her mother had not been so eager to march them into the nightmare awaiting them.

ꙮ

Grainne hated the convent. She hated it so much that she would only speak of the eight months she and her mother spent there once more in her life, and then never again after that.

When they had arrived on the doorstep of the convent later that morning, the nuns greeted them with much the same sort of the interrogation as the woman at the asylum had. While she had not been the friendliest of sorts, the nuns with their habits and wimples seemed much more frightening to Grainne. It did not help that they always seemed to have a rather dour disposition, always frowning, always chastising, always finding her at fault for something. In particular, she did not like the way Sister Clare looked down on her, always judging her for something, but she did not know what. She and her mother had been forced out of their home with nowhere to go, and so they had come here seeking refuge. What was so wrong with that?

"Sister Claire, aren't nuns supposed to help people in need?" she had asked her one day. She did not know if it was bravery or the fact that she was just tired of it all that had spurned her to do it.

"Of course," Sister Claire had replied. "It is our Christian duty to help others, particularly those most in need."

"Then why do you seem to hate us so?"

The question rang out in the classroom that Grainne had been forced to attend each day for catechism. The other children watched in rapt silence. Sister Clare glared at her. Then, quick as a snake, she leapt from her place behind her desk and had Grainne's arm in a vice-like grip.

"How *dare* you ask such a thing!" Sister Clare shouted at her, and before Grainne knew it, she had struck her across the face.

Blood rushed to Grainne's cheeks. No one in her short life had ever dared raise a hand to her like this before, not even her own mother, let alone ever beat her. She had vowed then and there that no one ever would again.

Grainne didn't tell her mother what Sister Clare had done when she saw her later that afternoon. They were only allowed to see each other for one hour a day under the careful eye of Sister Clare or, if they were lucky, under the more sympathetic supervision of Sister Bridget, and she did not want to cause her mother to worry.

The move to the convent had not been any kinder on her mother than it had been for Grainne. During the days, her mother worked in the laundry attached to the convent. The work was gruelling and depressing. Although she did not say it, Grainne noticed how much weight her mother had lost in the weeks since they had arrived, how she jumped at the slightest of sounds now, how she seemed to shrink under the watchful glares of the nuns. Her mother's hands, once smooth and delicate, had become red and calloused with work, her skin smelling of lye soap. It was not that her mother was not used to hard work – she had been a maid in Grainne's father's house before she had become a mother – but there was something so denigrating about working in the Magdalen laundries that seemed almost to break her spirit. It was confusing and heartbreaking for a girl Grainne's age to understand, so she began to drift away from her mother, as if she were afraid that was happening to her was catching.

"How are your lessons? Are you doing what the Sisters tell you? Are you behaving?" her mother would ask her every day.

"Of course, Mama," she would reply automatically, almost wishing the hour away. Of course, she hated her lessons, but she did not want to tell her mother that. She seemed to have enough to preoccupy her mind. Grainne had always been smart; she had an aptitude for learning, particularly numbers. Her tutor had always praised her for the skill she showed in her maths lessons. But the nuns did not teach them maths, or much of anything other than what could be found in the Bible. It was boring for a bright mind like hers.

"Good…good…" Her mother's voice would drift off then, like she did not know what else to say or do and the two of them would sit in silence until their hour was finished. Grainne found these visits torturous, and she could not wait to escape to play with the other children.

It was a revelation for her to be around children her own age. The only people in her life before had been adults, so navigating the art of making friends was an entirely new experience for her. She could not say she had been particularly successful at it; the other children seemed to find her aloof or too shy, and so they avoided her, but she managed to fall in with a small group of girls who were more or less friendly towards her. It was difficult, after all, to form a connection when it was every child for themselves, as her encounter with Sister Clare had taught her, when none of the other children had stood up for her, afraid that the Sister might focus her attention on one of them next.

"You shouldn't make an enemy of Sister Clare," a girl named Fiona whispered to her at dinnertime. "Once you make an enemy of her, she'll never leave you alone."

"I'm not worried," Grainne replied with more bravery than she felt. "My mother and I won't be here for much longer."

Fiona laughed mirthlessly. "You won't be leaving here, not for as long as you live. You'll be just like the rest of us. You'll go from the school to the laundry, and then you'll die."

Grainne looked at her, uncomprehending. There was no way she was working the laundry like her mother. They were only staying here until her mother could find somewhere else for them to go.

"There are only three ways out of here," Fiona explained in the manner of someone whose patience is running thin. "One is for the nuns to find you work outside of the laundry, and since they make money from keeping us here, they've no reason to let us go.

"The other way is for someone to come and claim you. And the kinds of girls who end up in here, the ones like me, like you, your mother; well, we don't have anyone like that in our lives, do we?"

Grainne did not respond. They both knew Grainne did not have anyone coming for her, much as she might like to wish otherwise.

"And the third?"

"The third way is your death."

Grainne's confidence wavered.

"My father will come and get us," Grainne finally retorted, her tone haughty, her nose raised imperiously. She wished she believed it.

"That's what almost everyone says," Fiona laughed her joyless laugh. "Everyone's got someone on the outside they hope will come and save them, and yet, here they stay."

She made an all-encompassing gesture taking in the full hall of children eating their supper.

Grainne tried not to show any fear, any doubt. She could tell that people would prey on any hint of either here. And yet, she was curious about one option Fiona had not mentioned.

"What about escape?" she asked, her tone full of genuine curiosity.

"Escape?" Fiona asked, her tone incredulous. "There's no escaping this place."

ꙮ

Grainne and her mother had been with the Sisters for three months when they found out exactly why no one had escaped from the laundry before.

Grainne had been outside, watching the other children play when there was a stir near the front gate. Hearing the commotion, the children stopped and ran to the fence that separated the little enclosed stone courtyard from the front gate, but all they could see were the gardai bringing someone in.

"A runaway," Fiona stated. Even though she was scarcely more than a couple of years older than Grainne, Fiona always seemed to have an air about her that made her seem much older and wiser than her years.

Moments later, Sister Bridget appeared at the door to the courtyard. "Children, it's time to come inside. You're wanted in the refectory."

Grainne fell in line with the other children as they were ushered into the refectory. When they entered, the nuns had already gathered the women from the laundry and had them line up. Grainne saw her mother standing in line, and she wanted to run towards her, but her mother motioned for her to stay where she was. Grainne turned her attention to the front of the room where a young woman with tear-streaked cheeks stood with several of the nuns assembled behind her.

"Mary Sullivan," she heard Fiona whisper beside her, nodding in the direction of the young, sandy blonde-haired woman who was trying to stifle her sobs. Grainne thought she recognized the young woman; she had a baby with her who'd been adopted out to another family.

"Hold out your hand," Sister Clare commanded.

Mary glanced at her, frightened, and clasped her hands together. Sister Clare grabbed it and held it stretched out in front of her. Quick as the snake she was, she brought the hardwood rod down upon Mary's outstretched hand. The sound echoed throughout the silent hall, making them all flinch. Mary did her best to stifle her cries, and to her credit, only some whimpers escaped her lips. The sound of Mary's beating would haunt Grainne for years to come.

The nuns did not need to state their message, it was clear to everyone assembled: try to run away and you will face the same fate.

"She's lucky she only got away with a few slaps on the hand," Fiona said afterwards as they were getting ready for bed.

In that instant, Grainne let go of any hopes that she and her mother would be escaping this prison the same way Mary Sullivan had tried to do. Fiona had been right: she would be stuck here forever unless someone came to rescue them.

ꕤ

Grainne was surprised, therefore, five months later, when on one visit with her mother, her eyes had lit up in a way Grainne had not seen since they had come to this place.

"I have some great news!" her mother chattered excitedly, smiling a foolish grin. It was a kind of joy that made Grainne feel uncomfortable, for she did not know what had caused it, nor did it seem to be a normal kind of joy. Her mother's temperament had changed greatly since they had entered the convent: her moods swung from extreme highs to extreme lows, and Grainne did not like being around her when either occurred.

"What kind of news?" she asked, cautiously.

"We are leaving this place!" her mother whispered excitedly, looking over her shoulder every few seconds at Sister Clare, as if the nun may yet try to stop them from leaving if she were to find out.

"Mama…" Grainne started, wondering if her mother might now be experiencing visions along with her moods.

"Did ye hear me? We're leaving!" Her mother grabbed at her hand and Grainne desperately wanted to pull back from her but was afraid it might incite her mother to more madness.

"Mama, I don't understand."

"We're leaving this place, Grainne. We can put all of this behind us now."

"Are we going home?" she asked. She could not stop herself from being a bit hopeful that her father might have changed his mind, realized that he could not live without his Gracie.

"No. No." Her mother shook her head, and her expression became a little morose now. "We can never go back there."

"Then where will we go?"

"A place of our own." Her mother's mood seemed to dampen a bit now, and Grainne once more had a feeling in the pit of her stomach that made her wary of this new change in circumstances. "Now, go back to the dormitory and gather your things."

Grainne ran back to the dormitory, gleefully ignoring the Sisters' rule about running in the corridor. She hurriedly pulled out the suitcase from under her cot and checked that she had everything.

"And where do you think you're going?" Fiona asked her, watching her from the edge of her own cot.

"We're leaving!" Grainne wanted to shout it from the rooftops, but there was still a part of her that wondered if this might not all be a dream and she wanted to wait until she was outside of the walls of the convent, far from the Sisters' grasp before she let herself entirely believe that they were never coming back here.

"I told you; no one leaves here." Fiona's tone made it sound like Grainne was being silly or going mad.

"Well, my mam and I *are* leaving."

"And did you suddenly find yourself a fairy godmother, then? Or are the two of you planning to run away like Mary Sullivan?"

"I don't know…my mam just said that we were leaving, and we don't mean to be coming back."

Fiona looked at her skeptically. "Well, don't say I didn't warn you when Sister Clare sends the gardai after you both."

"You'll never see me again, that I promise you." Grainne raised her chin defiantly, determined that she would never see the inside of this place again, if it was the last thing she did.

ꕥ

Grainne never know how they got out of the asylum. Her mother never spoke of it. She only knew from Fiona's words at the beginning of her stay that it could only have been possible with the help of someone from the outside. Who their benefactor had been, she would never find out. She was only grateful that they had rescued them from that hateful place.

Chapter Three

She had thought it a pretty name before: Henrietta. It sounded distinguished, refined. In time, she would grow to despise it for everything it represented.

The cobblestones of Henrietta Street were lined with Georgian townhouses that were once the homes of Dublin's wealthy upper classes. Their former splendour was much faded now; the seventeenth-century brownstone houses had melted into drabness with time and age, and the grime of industry. The houses had been chopped up on the inside, their guts sectioned off into multiple small apartments to house dozens of families in a single building. Close to a hundred people could be crammed inside its walls. Most of the doors leading into the buildings were propped open in the warm summer air, giving Grainne a view inside to the iron ore red and crown blue painted walls of the front entrances. People's washing hung out of windows that had once looked into people's parlours and drawing rooms.

Grainne's mother was clutching her hand so tightly as they moved down the street that Grainne felt her fingers going numb.

She marched her past the men slouched against the brown brick walls, clutching their glass bottles of indeterminate contents; past the hard-faced women with their equally hard stares who took a moment to pause the banality of their lives to watch as Grainne and her mother came marching down the street.

"Is this it?" her mother asked the landlord as he showed them inside a small, one-bedroom flat.

It had once been a parlour or some other such room and was now divided into two smaller rooms. The first one contained their kitchen and sitting room, which was also the room where Grainne would sleep. A narrow metal-framed cot had been pushed up against the far wall near the sash window. A sliding door that did not quite close properly was all that separated the main room from the bedroom. Once-bright yellow and red paint coloured the walls through the fading white plasterwork, making them look now more like mosaics from a long-forgotten time.

"Look, I've got two other families looking at the place. Ye can take it or leave it," the man shrugged, not seeming to care if they did either.

Grainne's mother nodded reluctantly and handed over a packet of rent money to the man.

"Pay your rent on time at the end of every month, or you'll find yourself back on the streets," he warned before turning around and heading back down the stairs.

"Well, this is something, isn't it, Grainne?"

Through the half-open window, they could hear children playing on the street below.

"Why don't you go outside and play with the others?" her mother suggested. "I'll unpack and see about getting us some dinner."

Grainne was not sure what that might entail, but she was not looking forward to finding out. Her mother had never learned to be a good cook, having always had someone else to cook for her.

Grainne followed the sounds of the children outside. One group of children were playing with a skipping rope and singing children's rhymes off to the right of the front entrance. The other group was kicking a ball over the cobblestones, laughing and screaming as their mothers kept watch from the windows above. Feeling suddenly shy and unsure of herself, Grainne stuck near the front steps watching the game until one of the boys accidentally kicked the ball over in her direction.

"Can ye toss it back?" the boy asked, approaching her. He was tall and skinny with a shock of auburn hair and a grin that would instantly charm even the frostiest person.

"Miss?" he asked when she did not instantly respond.

"Sorry?"

"The ball." He nodded to it resting at her feet. She bent down and picked it up, holding it out to him.

"I haven't seen ye here before… you just move in?"

She nodded.

"Paddy O'Reilly's the name." The boy stuck a dirt-stained hand out towards her.

She looked down at the small hand calloused by manual labour, even though he was still shy of his teenage years. Dirt and grime were embedded in his nails, the kind of grime that simply would not wash away no matter how long or hard you scrubbed for. It was the kind of grime life flung at you constantly when you lived in a place like this.

"Grainne."

She did not like being called Grainne; only her mother called her that. It was a name from her mother's people, a remnant of a near-forgotten language she would never learn. She had always much preferred being called Gracie, the name her father had always called her, but she was no longer that person anymore, and she never would be again.

"Grainne."

It did not sound so bad coming out of Paddy O'Reilly's mouth. Less irksome, somehow. Less scolding or cajoling. It still did not sound musical like other Irish names – it was too short and heavy-sounding for that – but nonetheless he made it sound almost pretty to her ears.

"Nice to meet ye."

She took his hand, ignoring the grime, and clasped it in her own delicate one. She did not know why, but she immediately felt safe around Paddy O'Reilly.

"You're welcome to join us." Paddy indicated the lads behind him who were cajoling him for holding up their game. She shook her head.

"I don't know how to play."

"Well, I can teach ye." He smiled kindly at her.

She shook her head again. "I'll just watch."

Paddy shrugged. "Suit yerself."

He returned to the game. She watched them play for the better part of an hour before her mother called out to her from the window above for their dinner.

"See ye 'round, Grainne," Paddy called to her as she headed inside. She did not know why, but it made her happy that he had noticed her.

Later that night, as Grainne lay in bed listening to the strains of different types of music permeating the thin walls, she felt a sense of peace wash over her. Down the street, someone was singing a beautiful opera in a strange language she had never heard before and, drifting down from the O'Reillys' flat above were the strains of a fiddle and an accordion. This was not the home she had grown up knowing before, but it was better than the convent.

At least here, she could feel safe.

ဢ

"Are ye lookin' fer something?"

Grainne looked up the question. It came from a girl not much older than herself. She recognized her from the day before when they were out playing in the street: Paddy's younger sister, Maureen. She was glad of a friendly face.

"We need water," Grainne replied. "I woke this morning to find that we don't have running water in our flat."

Maureen chuckled, dryly. "None of us has running water. The only water's in the basement. Come on, I'll take ye."

Grainne began following her down the corridor. Suddenly, Maureen turned around.

"Did ye forget something?" she asked, looking down at Grainne's hands.

Reflexively, she looked down and then back up at her. "What do you mean?"

"Did ye plan on cupping the water in your hands and bringing it up that way?"

Grainne suddenly felt very silly. She had not had to think of things like this before. She just expected there would be pails there for her to use.

"Come with me."

Maureen headed up towards the O'Reillys' flat. The higher they climbed, the steeper and narrower the staircase became. While Maureen went through the partially opened door, Grainne hovered in the doorway.

"Don't just stand on the step. Come in." Maureen beckoned to her. "Mam! We have a guest!"

Grainne stepped through the partially opened door into the parlour/kitchen. Physically, the O'Reillys' flat was much like the one she and her mother shared below. The walls were whitewashed to cover the plasterwork, just like in her own flat below. A border ran around the top of the room where it met the ceiling, a former ornate design with fiddles and flutes, and other musical instruments that had been plastered over, but whose shapes poked through now and then. The floors were scuffed and scratched from years of furniture and shoes. The flat had very much the same layout as hers, except the second room where her mother had her own bedroom was divided into two smaller rooms, one for Paddy and his siblings, the other for his parents. But it was not the layout Grainne noticed so much as the fact that it looked lived in; it was a *home*. The everyday bric-a-brac of life was scattered around the place. An old accordion sat on a chair, as if it had been placed there only a moment ago. Shoes were stacked by the door in a haphazard fashion. A clothesline was strung kitty-corner across one corner of the room near the fireplace, hanging from two nails that had been driven through the plasterwork. The fireplace was made of stone, the paint that once decorated it long gone.

A young woman about her mother's age stepped out from one of the bedrooms carrying a baby in her arms.

"Hello there, dear. And who might ye be?"

"Grainne."

"That's a pretty name." Mrs. O'Reilly smiled at her.

"Here." Maureen handed her a metal pail. "Ye can borrow this one until ye get one of yer own."

"And where are the two of you off to?" Mrs. O'Reilly asked.

"Just showing Grainne where to get water. She and her mam just moved into the flat below."

"Oh, well, welcome to our home."

"Thank you. And thank you for letting me borrow this. I promise to give it back as soon as I can."

"'Tis no trouble at all. If you or your mam need anything to help ye get settled, ye just come on up here and let us know."

Grainne smiled at her, surprised by the generosity of this family she'd only just met, but who'd been so kind to her without even thinking about it.

"Come on, I'll show ye the basement." Maureen brushed past her, heading back towards the stairs.

"How many of you live in here?" Grainne asked, curious, as she followed her out.

"There's seven of us. My mam and da, Paddy, myself, the twins, and the baby."

"And you all live in there?" Grainne was shocked. She couldn't imagine having siblings, let alone having them all crammed in together like that.

"Sure, and do you not have any siblings yerself?"

"No, it's just me."

Maureen looked at her with what Grainne thought might be pity, but also with maybe a bit of jealousy.

"That must be grand!" Maureen exclaimed. "I've always wanted to be an only child."

"Actually, it's kind of lonely," Grainne admitted, surprised at this revelation.

A silence fell between them for half a flight.

"And your da? Is he here too?"

Grainne paused on the stairs. "No."

Maureen looked at her but did not ask any more probing questions, seemingly understanding that it was not something she wanted to talk about just yet. Grainne took a moment to look down towards the basement and back up at how far they had come down.

"You mean to tell me that you bring up water every day all this way?"

"More than once a day," Maureen chuckled.

"Why do none of the flats have a bathroom in them?" Grainne asked a different question. She had noticed that the O'Reillys' flat had not had one either which, she supposed, was part of why they had to bring up so much water.

"Ye have a chamber pot under the bed, do ye not?" Maureen asked, seemingly astonished.

Grainne nodded, but the look on her face must have indicated that she hardly thought this sufficed.

"Well, there's the lavatory at the end of the corridor on our floor, and another on the first floor. And there's the lavatory outside in the yard as well. Although, it gets real dark at night, so if ye have really have to go in the night, you're better off just using the pot."

Grainne had never had to share a lavatory before. There had been plenty of them in her father's house; no one had ever needed to share them, except for the servants. It had never crossed her young mind until now that she and her mother were now on the same level as the help.

"And what about a bath?"

"There's a bath in the lavatory downstairs, and one in the one out in the yard as well. Bath day is usually Saturday so we're all clean for church on Sunday. Mind you, ye'll want to queue up early for it, though. Ye don't want to be the last one in with the water from everyone before ye."

Grainne's face paled at the thought of washing herself with other people's dirty bathwater.

"If I was you, I'd try and get into the one at the end of the corridor as it gets real cold in the winter. Ye're like to freeze to death before ye're cleaned."

"You mean to tell me that you have a bath only once a week?" Grainne asked, still fixated on this revelation.

Maureen looked at her, perplexed. "How often do ye need a washing up?"

The way she asked it, Grainne did not think it would be polite to tell her that she had had a bath every night before bed at her father's house.

They had finally arrived at the basement floor. Well, it was not so much a proper floor as old flagstones in some areas, but most of it was simple dirt. The girls went about pumping the water into their pails. They were engrossed in the task so much that they did not hear the creak of the stairs behind them.

"Boo!"

Both of them screamed, dropping their pails, water sloshing over the edge onto their shoes and splashing the flagstones.

"You two should see your faces," Paddy wheezed with laughter, his tall, thin frame shaking with mirth.

"Mam'll tan your hide for this, Paddy O'Reilly!" Maureen yelled at her brother. "You've only gone and caused the water to slosh all over us!"

Paddy sauntered down the last couple of steps to the dirt floor and stood before them. "I'm sorry."

Grainne saw he meant it, though that did not stop him from still taking pleasure in having given them both a fright.

"Come on, Mam said I was to help Grainne carry the pails upstairs." He bent down and picked up the heavy pail with ease, even though he scarcely looked stronger than Grainne herself. He turned back towards the stairs, expecting the two of them to follow.

"Ahem!" Maureen cleared her throat. "And what about this one?"

"You're well and used to carrying water up the stairs, Reenie. I'm just doing this as a favour to Grainne as she's a lady and not used to such work. Sure, and she's not the same as the likes of us," he retorted.

It had been an off-handed comment; nothing mean had been meant by it, but it still stung all the same. She *wasn't* like the O'Reillys, and she never would be. She did not belong here, and she was not sure she ever would. She must have had a look on her face for Maureen snapped at her brother.

"Sure, and look what you've gone and said now, Paddy O'Reilly!"

Paddy turned around and looked down at her. His young face creased with worry and he took a step down so that he was on the stair just above them.

"I didn't mean to upset yet, Grainne. I just meant that you're not a tenement rat like the rest of us."

"Rats?" Grainne's head whipped up at the mention of the word, snapping out of her brief melancholia. "There's no rats here…are there?"

The O'Reilly siblings shared a look and chuckled, like they were not sure if she was being serious or not. She paled to think that they might not be joking with her.

ꕥ

Grainne and her mother had been living in the tenement for scarcely a month when she would find out that, in fact, there *were* rats in the tenements.

"Ach!" Grainne made a noise that was halfway between a scream and a noise of disgust as a particularly large one ran over her shoe and out into the corridor past her as she had been coming home from school one day. She watched fearfully as she saw it scurry down the corridor and out of sight into some hidey-hole.

"What are you doing standing in the door like that? Come inside and shut the door behind you! I didn't raise ye in a barn," her mother snapped testily at her. Her mother was always testy these days. It had not been as easy to find work as she had been hoping, and the two of them were ever filled with the worry that they might forced to go back to the Sisters if they could not pay the rent.

"A…a rat!" she exclaimed, her face pale.

"What?!" Her mother screamed, pulling her dressing gown tightly around her, her eyes darting around the room. Unfortunately for the both of them, the rat decided to dart its way back from its hidey-hole in the corridor and into their flat again.

"There!" Grainne yelled as it scampered past her again.

"I *told* you to close the cursed door!" her mother screamed at her as she climbed up onto the table.

Grainne was stung by her words; her mother always seemed to find her at fault for something since they had come out of the convent. Without saying a word, she closed the door behind her trapping both her mother and the rat inside and headed up towards the O'Reillys' flat. She pounded on the door until Paddy let her in.

"Where's the fire?" he asked her, that look of slight amusement always present on his face.

"A rat!" she exclaimed, out of breath from bounding up the stairs.

The smile faded from Paddy's lips and he nodded to her, immediately understanding what she meant.

"You little witch!" her mother screamed at her when she opened the door to the flat again a moment later. "You left me inside with the cursed thing!"

"Ma'am," Paddy greeted her mother as if it was the most normal thing in the world to find her standing on the kitchen table in her dressing gown. "I hear ye've a rat that needs taking care of."

Her mother simply pointed to the bedroom. Paddy nodded and headed inside, shutting the partition doors behind him. Grainne heard a loud *thump!* a few seconds later, and the sound of the window opening.

"It's all taken care of," Paddy assured them, coming around the table to help her mother down. Grainne did not want to think about how it was taken care of.

"Have ye a mason jar or a glass ye no longer need?" he asked them.

Grainne grabbed the nearest jar off one of the shelves above the little fireplace and handed it to him. Paddy took the top off, put the jar on the ground and stepped on it with his boot, crushing it under foot. Carefully lifting the broken pieces, he wrapped them in a bit of cloth from his pocket and began shoving them in the hole where the rat had come out of.

"There," he said, brushing his hands carefully of the tiny splinters of glass. "That'll keep them out as best it can. They won't eat the glass, ye see, so they won't be like to come back this way lookin' for food again."

Her mother silently nodded to him in thanks and cautiously retreated into her bedroom, closing the door behind her.

"Thank you, Paddy."

"Sure, and it's no bother," he assured her. "And Grainne?"

She looked up at him.

"If ye ever need to, ye can always come 'round to ours. If things at home gets a bit much. You're always welcome." He nodded in the direction of her mother's room.

She nodded to him, grateful.

ꕥ

She would find herself spending a lot of time with the O'Reillys, especially now the damp chill of winter had begun to settle over Dublin.

"You're going to want to find something warmer than that," Paddy told her, looking down at her dress.

Grainne looked down at herself. She was starting to outgrow the pretty silk dresses and summer coat her father had bought for her, but she had nothing else to wear. They were the only worldly possessions she had, the only memories of her former life.

"And what about them?" she asked, nodding to some of the other children, still playing barefoot in the street despite the chill. "Have they no shoes to wear?"

Paddy shrugged. "There's fourteen in the Monaghan family to feed. Shoes are probably not something they could afford this month."

He looked back at her and seemed to note the concern on her face.

"We've all gone barefoot at one time or another," he said, seemingly in an effort to reassure her. "If none of us in the other flats has a spare pair to give them, I'm sure their da or mam will have appealed to the Church. The last thing they wants is for good Catholic families like us to be going to the Protestants for help. Although, if ye are ever in a pinch for something, the Protestants are like to help ye out. Though, mind you, they'll try to save your heathen soul."

He laughed teasingly.

Grainne did not think it would be polite to point out that *she* was a Protestant, even if she had not been to church in a very long time, and therefore, was not particularly worried about them trying to save her soul. Besides, she figured that keeping food on the table and a roof over her head were going to be of far greater worry for her than where her soul was like to go when she died, since her mother still had not found any work.

She shook her head a little in amazement, always surprised by the happiness the other tenants felt, despite the uncertainty of finding work and putting food on the table each day.

"You're all just so…happy." Her tone was full of wonderment.

"Of course, we are!" Paddy exclaimed, as if the statement was a little absurd. "We've a roof over our heads and food in our bellies. Most of the time, anyways. I don't like school so much, but Mam says we're lucky we get to go as there's folks who can't afford to send their children to get an education, so I s'pose we must be grateful for that as well. We've got each other, so what wouldn't we have to be happy about?"

"I don't know…Don't you ever wonder if there's any kind of better life out there?" she asked.

"C'mon," he gestured to her, trying to distract her from her thoughts. "It's about time to go 'round to the Gallaghers' place."

"What are we going to do there?" Grainne asked, pulling her thin jumper around her shoulders ever tighter.

"They've enough to keep their fire going all day long," he replied, always seemingly shocked that Grainne still had no concept about the daily life of living in a tenement, even though the O'Reillys had had to show her practically everything about how to survive Henrietta Street so far. "Mrs. Gallagher lets us stay in her sitting room a bit if we let her teach us some lessons. We can keep warm in there for a time."

Grainne did not much care what kind of lessons she had to learn; she just wanted to be able to feel her fingers and her toes again, so she followed him and a few of the other children up the stairs to the first floor. Her teeth chattered as another draught blew through the building. The main entrance doors in the front and back of the building were kept open all year round, so as to let people move easily between the streets on either side. This meant that the air inside the building was heavy and damp in the summer times and would freeze you down to your bones in the winter.

"Come in, come in." Mrs. Gallagher beckoned to them.

The children straggled in from the cold and immediately headed for the fireplace to warm their fingers.

"You're the new girl from down the hall, aren't you?" Mrs. Gallagher asked her. "You moved in with your mam not too long ago."

Grainne nodded.

"Well, you're welcome here any time. Many of the children come here, especially during the colder months, and you're welcome to join them."

Grainne smiled at her, grateful for the kindness.

"Now children, let's bring out your lessons and get a start on that homework, shall we?"

"Mrs. Gallagher teaches at the Protest school down the road," Paddy informed Grainne as they came over to the small dining room table and pulled out their lesson books.

Paddy soon lost interest in the lessons and was often found staring out the window most days rather than focusing on the lessons Mrs. Gallagher was helping them with. Grainne, however, loved the extra lessons and she was glad of the opportunity to once again have an unofficial tutor in Mrs. Gallagher.

"You're a clever one, aren't you?" she would say to her when Grainne would return all the maths problems she gave her with all the right answers in half the time of the other children.

"I like maths," Grainne replied simply, while the other children looked at her like she was off her rocker. "It's orderly…it just makes sense."

"Well, we'll have to come up with some more challenging lessons for you then, won't we?"

Grainne spent her winter days companionably between the O'Reillys and the Gallaghers now. She did anything to avoid coming back to her own flat until well after dinnertime. She would rise early in the mornings before the sun and would head out with the other children to school, and then she would come home and go straight up to the Gallaghers to warm up and to finish all her school lessons, and then it was off to the O'Reillys' flat for her dinner. She would sneak in before her mother came home and would settle into the little cot by the window and try to sleep before her mother and whatever gentleman caller she brought home with her arrived.

There was a constant parade of men coming and going from her mother's bedroom these days. They would come in loudly, usually waking her from a dead sleep, then move noisily through to the bedroom, slamming the partition door behind them. Grainne did her best to fall back to sleep quickly and ignore the creak of the box spring and other unidentifiable sounds coming from her mother's bedroom. The men would always leave before the dawn, stumbling through the living room, inevitably knocking something over and muttering bad words under their breaths. She would lie so still in the dark, praying they would hurry and be on their way, and allow her to fall back asleep again before she would have to rise for school.

There would always be a wad of cash on the table in the morning after they had gone, and Grainne would sneak some to buy food from the market on Moore Street on her way home from school to bring with her to the O'Reillys. She did not like depending on them for charity and she wanted to contribute to a family who had given her so much and asked for so little in return. They never asked her where she got the money from, even though everyone knew her mother had yet to find herself work. Grainne was grateful that the rules of society determined that one simply should not talk of such things.

It fell to Grainne now to take care of a lot of the tasks associated with the household. She had to do the washing up, the laundry, and cleaning, and paying the landlord the rent every month when he came by. Her mother, it seemed, had lost all interest in doing such things herself. Most of the day she would sit in her bedroom in her nightgown, often not even bothering to get dressed until it was near dark. She would sit there on her bed, smoking her cigarettes, one after the other, staring blankly through the haze of smoke out the dirty window that looked onto the street. She would only make an effort to rise from her stupor in the evenings after suppertime and would put on her make-up and a pretty dress, go out for a couple of hours, and then come home with a fancy man for the evening.

And so, the rent and food was paid for, and Grainne and her mother never talked about where the money came from.

ꕥ

Dublin
1950

One day, Grainne woke and found a subtle shift in the air. The icicles on the windowsill were melting, the little bit of snow that had been falling the last week had gone a muddy brown slush, and there was almost a different smell or taste to the air now. Like the other women of the tenement, Grainne had come to feel and recognize these subtle changes in the seasons over the last three years as well she knew how to tell the time of day without a clock. Sure enough, as she went down to the basement to fetch some water, she found a queue of women and girls with their buckets and scrub brushes in hand, ready for the first spring clean of the year.

"Ye could eat yer dinner off that!" Mrs. O'Reilly announced proudly an hour later, tossing her scrub brush back into the pail and standing up to admire her work. Grainne still was not sure how the women could really tell that the section of scratched and worn stairs they were responsible for were clean, but they seemed satisfied, and so Grainne was content to believe them.

"Come on girls; let's get the washing done."

She followed Maureen and Mrs. O'Reilly down into the yard where the other women were already doing their washing. There was always a genial banter that filled the courtyard when they did the washing, but today Grainne was quiet, reflective, as she took notice of the changes in herself since she had come to live at Henrietta Street. She had shot up several inches in the last couple of years, a hint at the height she would grow into as a young woman. Gone was the baby fat in her cheeks, and a determined jawline emerged. There was a certain hardness to her grey eyes, a steeliness that had set in. Her pale skin was either dirty from the grime of the street, or red and cracked from the lye soap used for all their washing and bathing. Grainne found that she did not really remember her life before the tenement anymore. The dull drudgery of daily eking out an existence had nearly drilled it out of her. She only remembered that it had been kinder, friendlier… *easier.*

If the years in the tenement had not been exactly kind to Grainne, they had been even harder on her mother. While still a pretty woman, it was noticeable to all how her mother had begun to waste away. The cigarettes and the booze that were the only thing she consumed now were not enough to sustain her. The dressing gowns that she had once filled now hung loosely over her frame, always slipping off her thin, bony shoulders to expose the sharp edges of her collarbone. Her grey eyes, once so bright and lively, were now hollow and blank; her once golden hair hung thin and limp down her back.

The men who had once visited with such regularity came around less often now. Her mother had been like a shiny pearl to them, her lustre drawing them in, but now they only saw tarnished gold plate that was beginning to fade. Grainne could not say she blamed them; she still spent most of her days with the Gallaghers or the O'Reillys so she would not have to look at the person her mother had become.

She supposed that she was meant to be sorry about abandoning her mother for the comforts of the O'Reillys and the Gallaghers, but then again, she had never really loved her mother, nor did her mother love her. She was obligated to keep a roof over her head, put food on the table, and send her to school, and so money was provided to take care of these obligations, but obligation was not the same thing as love, and they both knew it.

A certain resentment had set in between mother and daughter that would not budge. Although still young in age, the convent and the tenement had made Grainne wiser than her years, and she had come to piece together exactly how it was she and her mother had ended up where they were now. She felt ashamed of her mother; shame for what she had become, and shame for the life she forced her daughter to live now.

"Why did you do it?" she had asked her mother one particularly rainy day. The twins had caught a nasty cold that was going through the O'Reillys' flat like wildfire and Paddy had warned her to stay away, not wanting her to catch it too. Mr. and Mrs. Gallagher had gone to the suburbs for the weekend to visit her ailing father, so Grainne was cooped up inside the tiny flat alone with her mother.

Her mother did not say anything, nor did she look in her direction to acknowledge that she had even heard her daughter's question, although Grainne knew from the set of her shoulders that she had.

"If you didn't want me, then why didn't you let the Protestants have me when we went to the asylum?"

Her mother simply sat on the edge of her bed, staring out of the window at the dreary weather, the smoke from her cigarette tracing a long line up to the ceiling.

"You think you would have been better off at the asylum, do ye?" her mother finally spoke. She chuckled mirthlessly.

"Anything would have been better than that God forsaken convent." Grainne sat at the tiny table in the kitchenette, staring coldly at her mother.

"I kept you safe in that convent."

Grainne felt rage beginning to bubble beneath the surface at the memories of what she had gone through in the convent. She had forgotten most of the actual details of her time spent in the convent now; she had buried them down so deep inside her that only the emotional scars now lingered. But those scars burned every day with hurt, resentment, and rage.

"Safe? I saw you for an hour a day if the nuns were feeling generous, which was almost never, God damn their uncharitable souls. You could barely hold yourself together, let alone look out for me. *I* looked out for myself."

"You have no idea what I did, what I went through, to keep us safe in there." Her mother's tone was as cold as the rain pounding against the foggy windowpane.

"You've never done a damn thing for me!" Grainne screamed at her, her emotions finally getting the better of her. "If you hadn't taken me from my home, I wouldn't have had to live in that hellish nightmare, nor would I have had to move to this hellhole! You have only brought us pain and misery and ill fortune. At least if you'd left me in the asylum I might've…"

"Might've what?" her mother turned and rounded on her now. "Been taken in by some good Protestant family? You think they'd have really been better than what you have now?"

"Anything would be better than what I have now," Grainne snapped.

"Oh no my dear. You think you're all grown up now, that the convent and the tenement are the worst things in life you could see. You know nothing of heartache and pain and suffering. Not yet, but you will. One day." Her mother turned back towards the window, dismissing her once more.

Grainne seethed at her mother's curse. She was a hateful woman who had only loved one person in the world, and when he had abandoned her, she had had no more love in her for anyone else. Grainne made a pact with herself that she would never love anyone as much as her mother had loved her father. She would never let a man consume her, and so she would always remain the glittering diamond she knew she was. She would remain beautiful, but hard. Hard to the world; hard to love and be loved.

ꕥ

Grainne was nearly twelve when her mother finally died. Whether it was the cigarettes, the booze, or the melancholia of abandonment, she did not know. She found that she did not really care. She had bigger issues to worry about, like what she was going to do now that she was essentially an orphan.

She did not suppose her father would take her back, not that she would even know where to begin to look for him. It had been years since she had seen him; she was not even sure she knew the way back home anymore. Like it or not, her life was here now. There was no point in wishing it were otherwise.

Grainne cursed her mother for dying before she had reached the age of majority. At least then she might have been able to live on her own. As it was, she would have to find someone to take her in, or the Irish State would find a place for her. As it turned out, this very thought was also on the minds of the other families in the tenement.

"Well, we can't very well leave her on her own. She's like to be sent to the orphanage, or the laundries. I wouldn't wish either for her. She's too old to be adopted by a good family now, and any of the other families will just put her to work, or worse."

Grainne lay in Maureen's bed in the O'Reillys' flat, Maureen snoring softly beside her, listening to Mr. and Mrs. O'Reilly talking in low voices to the Gallaghers in the next room. She dreaded to think about being sent to an orphanage, or worse, back to the convent to work in the laundries. Although she knew she was stronger than her mother had been, Grainne was not so sure she would fare any better in the laundries than her mother had.

"She's a great lass, but ye know as well I, Aoife, that we can't take her in," she heard Mr. O'Reilly say. He sounded tired, having just come home from a long day working at the milliner's down the street. "We've five of our own to look after."

She heard Mrs. O'Reilly pause and she hoped beyond hope that maybe she would refute her husband's statement, that she would convince him to take her in. Until right now, Grainne had not realized just how much she wanted that. But no such denial came. Despite her best attempts, a tear slipped down her cheek and onto the pillow.

"We could take her in."

Grainne brushed the tear away, surprised to hear Mr. Gallagher speak up. He was a quiet man who often kept himself to himself, often working long hours at the chemist's shop he owned a couple blocks down the street. She had not seen him much in the few years that Mrs. Gallagher had been tutoring her after school, but on those rare occasions, he had seemed friendly enough. She had not dared to think that the Gallaghers might take her in before now. They were an older couple, in their mid-forties, with no children of their own. They were the only Protestants in the tenement but were well-respected by the other families. The thought of living them was enough to rekindle the tiniest flicker of hope in Grainne.

"Ye'd do that?"

There was a pause from Mrs. Gallagher and Grainne held her breath. She dared not move or breathe in case it might make them say no.

"We never thought we could have children before…it might be nice to have a girl about the place. And it will be nice to have some help in the chemist's shop on the weekends. What do you think?"

Grainne was not sure she liked the idea of working in the chemist's shop, but it was better than the convent or the orphanage. At least she would not be surrounded by complete strangers, and she would not be separated from Paddy or Maureen. She held her breath, hoping that Mrs. Gallagher would not refuse her husband's request. Grainne heard a mumbled response but could not quite make out what had been said.

"Well, why don't ye think on it until the funeral, and let's not say anything to her until you're sure. We don't want to get her hopes up."

It was too late, though. She was fully invested now in the idea of living with the Gallaghers, and she would do anything to make it happen.

ꙮ

"Surely there's something you'd like to say at your mam's funeral?"

Mrs. O'Reilly looked at her with kindness, but also expectation.

Grainne looked away from her, looking up into the faces of the small crowd assembled around her mother's grave, neighbours from the tenement, mostly. She did not know who exactly she was looking for at first, until she did not find him. She was surprised that she was stung by his absence. On the one hand, she had known her father would not come. After all, he had never once come looking for them in all the time since he had thrown them out and left them to the mercy of Dublin's streets. But she would have been lying if she had said that some small part of her had not hoped that once they had put the announcement in the papers about her mother's passing that he might read it and might care enough about them, about *her*, to come and say his condolences for a woman he had supposedly loved, and maybe spare a thought for the daughter who now only had the one parent left. But he had not come, and he would not spare a thought for her, Grainne knew. He probably had never spared a thought for her in all this time, probably only felt relief that she was no longer his problem.

"Grainne?"

She felt Paddy's gloved hand wrap itself around hers and she looked up at him. She was so grateful for him; she knew he was trying his hardest to make this easy for her.

She shook her head in response to Mrs. O'Reilly's question, and let the priest continue on with the burial rites, feeling that she was leaving behind a part of herself as she walked away from her mother's graveside.

Chapter Four

"This is the kitchen, and the sitting room, obviously." Mrs. Gallagher took her around their small flat, showing her where everything was even though she had been in the place almost every day for the last four years. "This is the bathroom, and this is our room. And this will be your room."

She paused in the open doorway of a small, spare bedroom. It had pale pink wallpaper with little violets on it. There was a small dresser near the window, a washbasin on a stand in one corner, and a bed that filled up most of the room. The bedspread was lilac, complementing the colour of the wallpaper. It was a very feminine room, and Grainne wondered if they had done it up especially for her. She liked to think so. It was small, and not much to look at, but it was better than sleeping on the cot in the kitchenette in her old flat.

The Gallaghers' flat was small, but cozy, and done up well. Grainne had been in the homes of the other tenants with their faded and peeling wallpaper, the indeterminate stains on the walls, and the rust around the taps of the sinks. There was none of that in the Gallaghers' flat; everything was clean and dusted and maintained. Grainne almost felt like she was afraid to touch anything lest she muss it up in some way.

"Thank you, Mrs. Gallagher." She turned around to smile at her. She wanted them to know she was grateful for what they were doing for her.

"Anne," Mrs. Gallagher replied. "You can call me Anne, if you like."

"Anne." She gave her another smile, not sure what else to do. She was not sure how she was supposed to act now that she was their ward.

"Well, we'll leave you to unpack. Supper is at six o'clock." Mrs. Gallagher turned towards her husband, leaving Grainne alone in the doorway.

She took a hesitant step towards the bed and laid her suitcase carefully upon the soft bedspread. She opened it and began to take out the few clothes and belongings she had, placing the stockings and underwear in a drawer in the dresser. She could not help but notice how pathetic they seemed lying there in the bottom of the drawer; they did not even fill up half of one drawer.

She moved then to hang up the three dresses she owned, the very same ones she had brought with her from her father's house. They were short on her now since her growth spurt. They were almost becoming too short to be modest anymore, but she had been too afraid to take some of her mother's money and go into a shop and buy herself new ones. She did not know the first thing about buying dresses or how much they cost.

She supposed that soon enough she would have to ask the Gallaghers to buy her new ones, or else she would have nothing but her shift to wear. Her mother had not left her much; just a watch and a bracelet she had taken with her when they had left the big house, along with her clothes. These were too big for Grainne just yet; she would not grow into them until she was a few years older. Grainne had taken what little was left of the money her mother had stored in the drawer beside her bed, most of which had gone to pay for her funeral, and she was not sure if there was enough left to buy new clothes or not. She was excellent with numbers, but she still did not really have a concept of money yet, just that she would need a lot more of it if she was going to make her way in the world. For that was what she intended to do now. She had spent too much time watching her mother waste away waiting for the one person she had depended on to look after her to come and rescue her. Grainne would never let herself end up in that position. She would become independent, with enough money that she would never have to rely on anyone for anything ever again.

The last thing she brought out of her suitcase was her stuffed rabbit, which she lay lovingly beside one of the pillows on the bed. The nuns had tried to take it from her at the convent, but she had managed to hide it away and keep it safe. It had become a bit ratty now and it had lost one of its eyes, but she still clung to it every night as one of the few reminders of her old life. Feeling suddenly tired, Grainne moved her suitcase from the bed and tucked it away in the corner of the closet, then lay down upon the bed. It was not long before she found herself drifting off to sleep, the past few days of grief and sleepless nights finally overtaking her.

ꙮꙮ

It was the morning of the next day before she woke. The scent of eggs and bacon sizzling in the pan wafted into her room from the kitchen. Grainne's stomach rumbled fiercely, and she was reminded that she had not eaten much in the last few days. Her grief and worry had kept hunger at bay, but now that she had let her guard down just a bit, her body's normal functions had become more apparent. She rose from the bed, splashed some cold water on her face, scrubbing it vigorously, as much to clean it as to wake herself up. She noticed how her dress hung limply from her, so she stripped herself down, changing into all fresh clothes. When she felt herself a little more presentable, she walked quietly towards the kitchen.

Mr. Gallagher was sitting at the table, the morning's paper in front of him and a wreath of cigar smoke encircling his head. Mrs. Gallagher was at the stove, serving up breakfast onto three plates.

"There she is." Mr. Gallagher's tone was friendly and inviting as he looked up from his paper and noticed her standing there.

"Good morning, Grainne," Mrs. Gallagher smiled at her. "Hungry?"

Grainne nodded.

"I thought you might be." She set a heaping plate of eggs, bacon, and toast down on the table, motioning for Grainne to take a seat and begin eating. She then placed a plate in front of her husband and laid one for herself. "You were sleeping so soundly last night we didn't want to disturb you for supper. We thought you might need the rest."

Grainne took a forkful of eggs and thought she had never tasted anything so heavenly in all her life. Mrs. O'Reilly had not been a bad cook in the years that Grainne had been taking her meals with the Paddy and his family; she just had not been a particularly inventive one. Grainne supposed that with so many children and a husband to look after, that she just simply could not be bothered to come up with anything more inventive than the usual because there would inevitably be one person who was unhappy with what got put in front of them. Grainne, however, was not going to boycott any meal Mrs. Gallagher put in front of her; not when it tasted this good. She made quick work of her plate, finishing up well before Mr. and Mrs. Gallagher had finished theirs.

"Hungry, were we?" Mr. Gallagher asked with a chuckle. Everything he said was almost always jovial in tone.

"Sorry," she apologized, realizing that it probably seemed rude of her to have eaten so quickly. She should have remembered her manners and eaten more delicately.

"No need to apologize, dear. I'm sure you were famished after everything that's happened this week." Mrs. Gallagher looked at her sympathetically, but not pityingly, for which Grainne was grateful. "Would you like seconds?"

Grainne thought about it a moment. On the one hand, her mind was telling her to take as much as she could now, in case they changed their minds and turned her out, but she also did not want to look greedy. In the end, appearances won out.

"No thank you. It was very good though." She smiled at them, hoping to convey as much goodwill as she could so they would never want to get rid of her.

"Well, you won't have to worry about going hungry here," Mr. Gallagher said with a smile. "Anne's the best cook this side of Dublin."

"Oh stop." Mrs. Gallagher blushed at her husband's compliment. "Now, Grainne, I was thinking that later today you and I could go into town and do some shopping. I noticed that your wardrobe could use a bit of filling, and I thought we might pick you up some new things. What do you think of that?"

Grainne looked at her, not sure what to think or say. "Are you sure it's not too much of a bother?" she asked, eventually.

"It's no bother," Mrs. Gallagher reassured her, warmly. "Sean will be going into the shop to open up, and you and I can continue on into town."

Grainne smiled at them both, grateful for all they had done for her so far, but also sad because she knew she could never be the kind of daughter they were hoping for.

***

Dublin
1955

Despite the warmth and kindness the Gallaghers had showed her, Grainne never quite settled into life with them. She always seemed to have one foot out the door, ready to leave in case they ever decided they no longer wanted her. She wanted to make sure she was the one to do the leaving, not the one being left out in the cold again. She knew it pained them that she always kept them at a bit of a distance, so she tried to make up for it in other ways. She had agreed to take on their surname when they took her in, not really wanting any part of her old life anymore. That Grainne had been a pitiable creature; Grainne Gallagher on the other hand, she was going to go places, or that was what she told Paddy every day.

She excelled at her school lessons, earning top marks in her classes, even earning herself a scholarship to help pay for her school fees. She also helped out in the shop on the weekends. While other teenagers her age were going off to the pictures or the park, or doing whatever it was that teenagers did, she was always working towards her goal of becoming self-sufficient, self-reliant. She pocketed away any earnings, always making sure not to spend it on silly things like sweets or new clothes unless she absolutely had to. Because of her maths skills, she worked her way up to helping Mr. Gallagher with the book-keeping for the shop. She learned about inventory and ordering new items, and kept up with the trends so that they always stocked the latest in-demand items. She was running math figures in her head at night, always trying to work out exactly how much she would need in order for her to get a flat of her own and work her way up in the world.

Grainne was not the only one trying to make their mark on the world. Just shy of his eighteenth birthday, Paddy decided to quit school.

"You're not coming to school today, Paddy?" Grainne had asked him, watching as he had hopped on the new bike he had brought home the day before.

"Can't," he had said, swinging a leg over it. "The newspaper up the road needs a messenger boy, and Mam could use the extra money. You lot get going now before you make me late for my first day."

She knew it had not been an easy year for him. Illness had struck the tenement particularly hard that spring, taking both Paddy's father and the twins. Mrs. O'Reilly had been beside herself for weeks. Grainne had visited every day, helping Paddy and Maureen with whatever she could, even if it was just to be there to have someone to talk to. But Grainne had never been good around emotional people, and always felt like she was in the way, and so she did her best to avoid Mrs. O'Reilly.

"What about the attendance inspector?" she had shouted at Paddy's retreating back as he had headed off to the newspaper, but he had gone out of earshot.

The attendance inspector had come around to the O'Reillys' flat looking to find out why Paddy was not in school, but after being told time and again that they simply needed the extra income, they had gotten tired of trying to force him back to school. The Gallaghers had been none too pleased to find out that Paddy had dropped out of school, nor about the new friends he had begun spending his time with now after work.

"Grainne, I think it would be best if you didn't spend so much time with Paddy these days" Mrs. Gallagher had said to her one day over supper.

Grainne had looked at her, confused. Paddy had been her constant companion since she had come to live at Henrietta Street, her best friend. The two had not gone a day without seeing one another, even now that he worked as a newsboy and she worked in the shop when she was not at school. They still somehow managed to find the time to talk every day, the highlight of her day.

"Why?" she had asked, her tone indignant.

"Sean and I feel…we just don't want you to end up with the wrong sorts of people, is all."

"But Paddy's my friend," Grainne had replied, her tone becoming panicked now at the thought of not being allowed to see him again. She did not know how she would have survived her years here without him, and she could not bear the thought of being separated from him.

"I know, and he's not a bad lad, but yours and Paddy's lives are heading down different paths now. The kinds of lads he spends time with… you just don't want to fall in with that sort."

Grainne did not know what to say to this, so she had not said anything. Mrs. Gallagher must have taken her silence for acquiescence for she let the matter drop. Grainne, however, was determined to find out from Paddy exactly what he had been up to that would make the Gallaghers feel they had to warn her off him. The next morning on the way to school, Grainne decided to ask his sister about it.

"Reenie, do you know anything about any new friends Paddy might have?" she asked, trying not to seem too conspicuous with her questions.

Maureen thought for a moment, twirling a strand of her auburn hair around her pencil as they walked. "No, not really. Oh, I s'pose there's the Dempsey boys and a few others from upstairs. D'ye mean them? He's taken to meetin' them after his shift and they go down to Temple Bar. Mam doesn't like it, but he says as he's the man of the house now, and he can do as he likes."

She shrugged, seemingly trying to stay out of any squabbles between her mother and her brother. She had become quieter since the passing of her father and younger siblings, more withdrawn of late. She was not the same boisterous person Grainne had first met when she had needed to be shown how to fetch water from the basement.

Grainne knew now what Mrs. Gallagher meant when she had said that she did not want her falling in with the wrong crowd. The Dempseys were known around the tenements to get into more than a lick of trouble. The gardai had caught them at thieving and other petty crimes on more than one occasion. Paddy had been known to get into his fair share of trouble now and then too, but he had never gone so far as criminal behaviour before, and she was ashamed that he would start now.

After school, Grainne turned out of the schoolyard, but instead of heading back home, she turned towards the River Liffey, heading in the direction of Temple Bar.

"Home's this way!" Maureen called to her, surprised to find her deviating from their usual path.

"I know!" she called back, continuing on her warpath. A moment later, she heard Maureen huffing as she jogged to catch up, falling into step with her. As they began to near the centre of town, it dawned on her where they were headed.

"Oh no," Maureen said, pausing a moment. "Ye can't mean to be going down to Temple Bar. Leave it be, Grainne. Paddy's just having a tough time of things of late, what with Da, and the twins, and him needin' to look after me, and Mam, and little Liam. He'll get bored of the Dempseys soon enough."

Grainne was not going to take that chance. Paddy might be grieving and dealing with it in his own way, but she was not going to let him become a criminal because of it.

She and Maureen got more than a few curious stares from punters stumbling out of the pubs along the river as they marched down the streets in their school uniforms, their lessons still in hand. Grainne ignored them and continued her brisk, determined pace until she rounded the corner and found them outside of *Murphy's* a few moments later. They were just in time to watch as Paddy and the Dempseys were looking for easy marks, working together to distract them so they could pick their pockets. She stood there, shocked, watching how he picked an older man's pocket with ease, like he had done it a hundred times before. She was brought out of her reverie by the arrival of Mr. Murphy himself, who had noticed what the boys were up to.

"Here now, what do you think you're playing at?" he roared in Paddy's ear, snatching him up by his collar. The Dempsey boys all scurried away like rats, leaving Paddy to take on the consequences of their actions.

"I'm sorry, sir. Please don't hurt me. Here's your change back. I didn't mean no harm, honest!"

"An honest thief, eh? What do you make o' that, Miller?" Murphy addressed the man Paddy had stolen from.

"Ah leave him be, Murphy; poor thing looks like he needs these few bob more'n I do." Miller handed the change Paddy had stolen from him.

"Right. Do ye have a family, boy?" Murphy addressed him sternly.

"It's just me mam, me sister, me little brother, and I."

"And where exactly does your mother think you are right now?"

"Probably at work or home."

Murphy observed him silently for a moment.

"Ye aren't going to hand me over to the gardai, are ye?" Paddy asked, his tone fearful.

"Do you want me to call them?" Murphy asked him.

"No sir! Please don't, sir!"

"Take it easy, lad. I'm not going to call the gardai. If Miller here doesn't want to press charges against you, I don't need to be either. I suspect ye did it more to impress those boys you were hanging about with?"

Paddy nodded.

"Well, we might not press charges, but we don't take kindly to thieves 'round these parts, so I expect you'll not be makin' a repeat performance of today."

"No sir."

"Good. Well, to ensure ye don't, I'm going to have ye come here and work for me."

"Work for you, sir?"

"I need another set of hands around this place to help out, and you clearly need to make some extra money. I think it's a good fit, don't you?"

"Yes sir, I mean, but ye don't know me. Don't I need qualifications?"

"Do ye know how to clean dishes and sweep floors?"

Paddy nodded.

"Then that's all the qualifications you need. Now get yourself back home. It looks like you've some people who've been lookin' for ye." Murphy nodded in Grainne and Maureen's direction.

"Grainne?" Paddy looked horrified, realizing that she was there.

She was so angry with him for having become a thief that Grainne didn't think she could even look at him anymore. She turned on her heel and began marching back in the direction of home.

"Grainne!" She heard Paddy jogging to catch up to her. "Grainne, I can explain."

"So, you've taken to thieving now, have you?" she asked, rounding on him.

"It's not like that…the lads were doing it as a bit of fun at first…"

"I don't care what the Dempseys do. I care about what *you* do, what kind of person *you* are, and I don't want to associate with thieves, Paddy O'Reilly."

Grainne walked briskly ahead, always keeping as much distance between them as she could. Paddy hung back respectfully, walking with his sister.

"Mam is *so* going to tan your hide for this," Maureen snapped at her brother before the three of them carried on the rest of their journey home in silence.

ᘎᘏ

Grainne refused to speak to Paddy for a week after that. It was the longest either of them had gone without seeing or speaking to one another. Grainne threw herself into her schoolwork and picked up extra hours in the shop, while Paddy was off doing God only knew what. She told herself that she did not care what he was up to, that he was no longer any concern of hers, but of course, it was not true. She thought of him every waking minute that they were apart, and she hated not being able to talk to him. It was all consuming, trying not to think of him. It was torture for her. Of course, she knew there was always the option that she could go to him and tell him what she was feeling, but they both knew she would never do that. She had never let herself be vulnerable with anyone, not even Paddy O'Reilly.

The first time she saw him all that week was after she was coming home one night from a late shift in the shop. It was the end of the quarter and she had stayed in late to finish up the accounts for Mr. Gallagher, assuring him that he could go home for supper and she would lock up. Grainne had never been particularly bothered by walking home in the dark, but that night, she could not shake the feeling that someone was following her, that something was just not right. She turned the corner into Henrietta Street, quickening her pace when she finally heard it: footsteps falling into pace with hers, and more than one pair of them. She quickened her pace once more but was stopped by the sudden appearance of a shadow in front of her.

"Well now; look what we have here."

Grainne stepped back, recognizing the voice as that of John Dempsey, and ran straight into the arms of his younger brothers who had been following her from behind. Strong hands gripped her upper arms, fingernails digging into her skin. No matter how much she tried, she could not shake them off.

"Stop struggling, girl. We just want to have a friendly little chat." One of the younger boys pushed her up against the brick wall of the tenement building, the three of them hemming her in so she had nowhere to run.

"Paddy won't hang 'round with us no more." John Dempsey got so close to her face she could smell cigarettes and Guinness wafting off his breath. She did not try to hide her revulsion at the sight or smell of him.

"That's nothing to do with me."

"Come now, Grainne, we both know that's not true. If he hadn't seen you that day outside Old Murphy's, then he'd not've stopped pickpocketing for us, and ye see, I can't abide that. He's one o' the best we got, a real natural ye see, and I'm going to need some reparations now you've taken him away from us."

Grainne raised her nose an inch or two into the air, staring down at John Dempsey. She was taller than him by a couple of inches, and she knew he was sensitive about his height, especially around her; he did not like being shorter than a girl. It made him feel inferior, and her looking down on him now only inflamed his inferiority.

"Ye know what the problem with you has always been? The problem with you Grainne Gallagher, is that you've always thought you were better'n us. Ever since that first day ye came to the tenements in that fancy silk dress, too pretty to play with the likes of us, your nose up in the air, looking down on the likes of us just like ye are now. Well, I think it's time we bring that nose down a notch or two, isn't it lads?"

"The problem with you, John Dempsey, is that you've never understood a thing about me," Grainne replied, her voice cold, not hiding the fact that she *did* think she was better than the likes of John Dempsey and his brothers.

She could see the fist coming towards her out of the corner of her eye. She did not flinch, just reacted. She brought her knee up between his legs, getting him right where it would hurt the most. Dempsey bowled over, screeching in both pain and surprise. His brothers, feeling a lot less bold now, did not know whether to carry on or flee. It only took them half a second to make their decision once Paddy showed up only a moment later.

"Hey! Get off her!" he shouted at them, and they sprinted off, leaving their ring-leader behind the same way they had left Paddy behind when he had been pinched by Mr. Murphy. Dempsey tried to regain his posture to run after them, but Paddy got to him first and punched him across the face. As he tried to pick himself up off the ground, Paddy gave him a swift kick in the arse, sending him sprawling onto the cobblestones.

"Paddy!" Maureen shouted at him from the window above where she and half the street were now watching the brawl. "That's enough."

Reluctantly listening to his sister, Paddy backed off and came over to where Grainne was still standing, frozen in place.

"Grainne?" Paddy brought his hands up to either side of her face. Still in shock, she batted his hands away and made to punch him, her instincts mistakenly perceiving him as another threat.

"Woah there," he said, his voice soft and low. He put his hands up and backed away slowly like she was some frightened animal. "Woah there. I'm not going to hurt ye, I promise. I just want to check that you're alright."

"I'm fine," she snapped. Paddy looked a bit hurt at her tone, but she could not bring herself to worry about that right now.

"Get away from her!"

Grainne looked up at Mrs. Gallagher screaming at Paddy. She wanted to tell her that it had not been his fault, that he had been trying to help her, but she could not seem to get the words out.

She felt a soft touch on her upper arm and a warm blanket was wrapped around her shoulders. She felt Mr. Gallagher's strong, reassuring arm guiding her back into the building, whispering how sorry he was, how he should never have left her alone to walk back by herself in the dark. She wanted to reassure him that she was fine, but her brain was starting to feel a bit fuzzy now, like she was dizzy, even though no one had struck her.

"You just stay away from her, Paddy O'Reilly. I don't want to see you around her anymore, do you understand?"

Grainne did not get to hear Paddy's response to Mrs. Gallagher's command as she was shuffled away to the flat upstairs.

ꟸ

After her encounter with the Dempseys, the Gallaghers would not let Grainne go anywhere alone, even in broad daylight. It annoyed her to have her freedom taken away for something she was not to blame for, but she knew they were just trying to protect her. After the initial shock had worn off and the adrenaline from her instincts had calmed down, Grainne's thoughts had cleared. She felt sorry she had reacted the way she had when Paddy had tried to help her. She wanted to go to him and apologize, but with the Gallaghers shadowing her every move, she knew they would not let her talk to him. She also suspected that Paddy was purposely avoiding her, coming and going from the tenement when he knew she would not be around. She did not even see Maureen all that week.

Finally, at the end of the week, there was a knock on the Gallaghers' door. From her bedroom, Grainne could hear muffled voices in what seemed to be a bit of an argument, and she was curious as to who it could be.

"Grainne? There's someone here to see you," Mrs. Gallagher called to her.

She hopped off her bed, put down the book she was reading, and came to the front door. When she saw who was standing in the entryway, she was torn between running towards him and turning on her heel and storming back to her room. She was still angry with him over the pickpocketing, but his attempts to rescue her from the wrath of the Dempseys had somewhat softened this anger.

"What do you want?" she asked, folding her arms across her chest, looking at him expectantly.

"I was hoping to talk to ye," he replied, cautiously. He looked behind her to where Mrs. Gallagher was standing in the kitchen. Grainne nodded to her, letting her know she would be fine to talk to Paddy for a few minutes. Reluctantly, she left the two of them alone.

"Well?"

"Look, I wanted to say that I'm sorry about the other day…that's not me, you know it's not. I was being an eejit, and I'm real sorry that John and the lads tried to take it out on you. I couldn't forgive myself if something happened to you, Grainne, because of me or something I'd done. I never meant for you to get hurt."

His face looked so serious, a look she had rarely seen on him before, that she wanted to reach out and reassure him, but something held her back. Instead, she said nothing, just stared at him, not because she was angry with him anymore, but because she did not know what to say in response to that.

"Oh, come on, Grainne," he pleaded.

"I'm waiting for you to tell me something I don't already know," she finally said, trying to seem imperious, her default tactic for dealing with any situation so that she could keep her guard up and not let anyone in.

He sighed. "I went back to Mr. Murphy, and to make up for what I've done, I'm going to be workin' for him now. It's just washing dishes before closing, but I don't care. I want to make up for what I've done, not just to him, but to you too."

She continued to stare at him.

"I'm going back to school," he told her, still trying to impress her. "Mr. Murphy says that I need to finish my learnin' if I'm to continue workin' for him."

He looked at her pleadingly, hoping that all of this would be enough, knowing that it would not be.

"C'mon, Grainne…can ye not find it in your heart to forgive me?"

She paused a moment before crossing the room and putting his face between her hands and kissed him. She had never kissed anyone before, nor had she been kissed, so she was not sure what to expect. All she knew was that the fairy tales that she had read where the prince kisses the princess were wrong. It was so much better in real life than those stories could ever describe. Paddy must have felt something similar, for he only pulled back when he reluctantly had to come up for air.

"Don't ever not talk to me again, Paddy O'Reilly, or hide away from me, even if someone tells you to," she told him firmly when she had caught her breath.

"*Me* not talk to *you*? I thought it was *you* who wasn't talkin' to *me*?" he asked, completely confused by the whole situation.

"Well, and so if I was, it was because you deserved it," she retorted.

Paddy grinned at her.

"God almighty, but you, Grainne Gallagher, are the most marvelous woman I've ever known. Confusing as hell, but marvelous."

ജ്ജ

Despite strong disapproval from the Gallaghers, Paddy and Grainne were never separated again.

True to his word, Paddy returned to school during the days, and in the evenings, he worked for Mr. Murphy. Mrs. Gallagher had reluctantly agreed to tutor him on weekends to help him catch up. Secretly, Grainne thought she was pleased with the efforts he was making, even if she did not want to show it. It did not leave him and Grainne much time for courting, but it was enough for now that they got to see one another again.

Paddy finished his schooling on time, and even planned to go to university in the autumn – in no small part due to some help from Mr. Murphy for the tuition – but things took a rather tragic turn before he had even had the chance to enrol. While working a shift, Mr. Murphy had collapsed and died of a heart attack. Having no other family, he had left Paddy the pub and what little money he had. Determined to do the best by the man he had come to regard as a second father, he had forgone his enrolment and decided to run the pub full-time.

"What does your mam think of you running the pub?" Grainne asked him one evening as the two of them sat in one of the booths after closing, taking in the enormity of how their lives were about to change.

"She's none too pleased about it," he admitted. "I think she'd really rather'd set her eyes on me being the first in the family to ever go to uni."

Grainne could not say she blamed Mrs. O'Reilly. Paddy running a pub had not really been in her vision of their future either.

"Sean and Anne aren't too pleased about it either." They had made that clear to her when they had heard the news.

"And what about you?" he asked, his tone curious but also a little hesitant, like he was scared of her answer. "What do you think of all this?"

She paused a moment, leaning her head against his shoulder, thinking over her response.

"It wasn't how I'd thought things would turn out for us," she admitted, staring around the place that was all his now. "But I don't know…there's something to be said about you being a businessman now of your own accord. There's respectability in that, I think."

He smiled down at her, evidently pleased that she did not, at least, hate the idea.

"I'm glad to hear ye say that, because I really want to run this place; do Old Murphy proud. I want to run it the way he did; like it was a safe haven for anyone dropping in, a place to give back to the community. I want it to be like a home for anyone who needs it."

A silence fell between them as they thought of what their new future was going to look like now.

"But you are going to change the name, right?" she asked him, suddenly.

"What d'ye mean?"

"Well, you can't very well be running a pub named *Murphy's* when you're not a Murphy," she replied, as is this was obvious. "It should be in your own name."

Paddy mulled this over a moment.

"*O'Reilly's*," he said, as if he could envision it written outside above the door. "Ye know, it has a nice ring to it." He smiled at her.

"What?" she asked him, wondering what the big, goofy grin on his face meant.

"I just never thought I'd ever have something of my own before. Something that was just mine, nobody else's. Ye don't know how rare that is when you grow up with five siblings."

"Well, get used to it, Mr. O'Reilly," she told him. "You're going places."

ꕥ

It was not long after Paddy had the pub up and running under its new name and ownership that he had come round to the Gallaghers to ask for Grainne's hand in marriage. Of course, knowing her perfectly, he had not asked Mr. or Mrs. Gallagher if he could marry their ward, but had gone straight to Grainne herself. Knowing that the only person in the world whose opinion she would listen to was her own, he had gone straight to her one night after a long shift at the pub and gotten down on one knee with a small, silver claddagh ring.

"I know it's not a diamond, and I know it's not much…"

"It's absolutely perfect," she assured him, gleefully admiring the ring on her finger. She was so happy in that moment that, for a short time, she allowed herself to dare to dream that maybe now she could be happy.

Chapter Five

Of course, as was the way of things, the dream never lasted for very long.

Neither the Gallaghers nor the O'Reillys were particularly thrilled with the idea of Paddy and Grainne marrying. They had expected it from the Gallaghers; they both knew what they thought of Paddy. But it was the O'Reillys who hurt both Paddy and Grainne with their rebuff the most. Paddy had always thought of Grainne as family, and he knew she thought of the O'Reillys in the same way. It had been especially painful then, when his mother and sister had rejected the idea of her joining the family.

The main problem, naturally, was that Grainne was a Protestant. While it had not mattered to Paddy which church his future wife attended, it was the only matter which seemed important to his mother.

"What d'ye mean she won't convert?" his mother had asked him not longer after they had announced the engagement.

"Ye can't be married in the Church if you're not both Catholics."

"We're not getting married in the Church, Mam." Paddy had tried to keep his tone even, hoping that it might keep her calm. Naturally, it had not worked. His mother's jaw had dropped open, astounded by this revelation. He had been putting off this particular conversation for days now for this very reason. He had mulled over the best way to bring up the subject with her, but there had never seemed to be a right moment or a right way to break it to her. The O'Reillys were God-fearing Catholics, always had been, and there would be no exceptions to this rule as far as Old Aoife O'Reilly was concerned.

"Well, why'd ye get engaged then, if ye can't be married? Ye can't be startin' a family with her without gettin' married, Paddy O'Reilly. I won't stand for it. We are respectable people, and that won't be changin' so long as I'm alive, ye hear?"

Paddy had sighed.

"We're still getting married, Mam, just at the Registry Office and not the Church."

Well, this news had sent her into even more of a tizzy and she went off in a huff, refusing to speak to him for weeks. It had taken great cajoling on the part of his sister, Maureen, to bring her around. When she did eventually come around – with great reluctance – he thought Grainne might have wished they had not worked so hard to include her in the wedding preparations.

"She's being intentionally contrary," Grainne had complained to him, coming into the pub one day on her lunch break from the shop.

"Who is, love?"

"Who else?" She gave him a pointed look.

Paddy did his best to look sympathetic. "We could always run away and get married."

He was only half-joking.

"Then she'd surely never talk to me again." A look came over her face then, like that might not be the worst thing in the world for her.

"Try not to look too pleased at the thought," he had begged of her.

"I'm only saying…"

"And I'm only saying that no matter how contrary she might be, she's still my mother and I still want her there when I marry the woman I love."

Grainne had twisted her mouth into a little moue and breathed in a long sigh. "Fine, we won't run off and get married, much as I'm beginning to like the idea."

"Thank you." He had leaned across the bar then and gave her a quick kiss, much to the amusement of the punters waiting on their pints.

His mother's attempts to be a hindrance in the wedding planning notwithstanding, everything was starting to come together on schedule until three weeks before the wedding. Mr. and Mrs. Gallagher had gone outside of the city to a wedding for one of Mr. Gallagher's nieces. One the way home, their car took a turn too fast along a dark and slippery stretch of road and the car overturned, killing them both.

"At least they say they were killed almost immediately. That's some small mercy," Maureen had said to no one in particular, just saying something for the sake of saying it.

Paddy had shot his sister a look, like the last thing she was doing was being helpful, but Grainne had not seemed to hear what Maureen had said. She had seemed numb since they had been told the news, which was to be expected, he thought. He knew what other people thought of her cool reaction to the news that her foster parents were dead, and she was left alone in the world once more. They saw her numbness and shock as her being aloof, uncaring and unfeeling, just as she had been at her mother's funeral. To anyone but him, it was as if she was completely unaffected, but he knew better. He could see the raw emotions bubbling just beneath the calm exterior, even if she would not discuss them with him. She was an orphan once more; no one was immune to that kind of tragedy, not even his brave Grainne.

"Can you even be considered an orphan if you're a grown woman?" she had asked him later, when he had taken her back to the Gallaghers' flat.

He had simply held her then, not knowing what else to do. He felt her shake a little, like she might cry, but she collected herself, still unable to breakdown even around him. She always had to be so put together all the time. It broke his heart to think of the effort it must take for her to do that.

"Will you stay here with me tonight?" she had asked, her voice small and thin, but calm. He knew it was her way of trying to let him in.

"Of course, love. Whatever ye need. I'm here for ye. I'll always be here for ye."

ꟷ

After the funeral for Sean and Anne Gallagher, Grainne had thrown herself into the last of the wedding planning, determined that everything should go on as she had originally intended. There were whispers about whether it was entirely appropriate not to postpone the wedding for awhile, considering it was scheduled for only a week after the funeral, but Grainne had decided that her former guardians would have wanted her to continue on with the wedding, and so that was what she intended to do.

And it was not just wedding planning they had to do, but planning for when they would move out of the tenement as well, for Grainne was determined not to live in Mr. and Mrs. Gallagher's flat, and there was certainly no room for them in the O'Reillys' flat. Not that Grainne would have ever considered that to be an option anyways.

"So where will the two of ye live, if not in the Gallaghers' place?" his mam had asked him after the funeral.

"Grainne's found us a flat in The Liberties until we can buy a house in the suburbs. She heard back about it just yesterday. We're to move in right before the wedding on Saturday."

"The Liberties!" his mother exclaimed. He might as well have said he was moving into Dublin Castle. "And how did the two of ye find a flat there? There's strict rules about who they let in."

"Don't I know it," Paddy had muttered, striking a match and lighting his pipe. It was one of the last times he was going to get to enjoy the simple act of smoking a pipe, since Grainne hated the smell of it, and he planned to take full advantage. "Ye have to be Protestant, for one. Thankfully, Grainne's one, and we'll just happen not to mention that I'm not."

He tried not to glance at the glowering look his mother was giving him, both for marrying a Protestant, and for lying to his new landlord and neighbours.

"And I have to stay off the drink," he added.

Exclamations of amusement and disbelief rose from those assembled.

"That'll be a fine thing for a publican," Maureen teased him, knowing he liked his pints just as much as the next person. He could not disagree. He did not know how he would do it, but if it meant that Grainne got her wish of not having to live in the tenements, then he would do it for her.

"The Liberties is bad enough, but the suburbs! Don't say ye'll go to there, Paddy," his mother had almost wailed. "I'd never manage if I never saw your face again."

"Mam, it's not that far away," he had replied, but knowing it would fall on deaf ears.

"Ye hear of folks moving out there and never being seen or heard from again," his mother complained.

In all the years he had grown up on Henrietta Street, there had been some families that had split up, with some moving out to the suburbs, chasing a better life and never came back again. It was expensive to take the bus back into the city from places like Finglas they knew, just like they knew that if Paddy and

Grainne moved out there, they would be just like those other families that never came back.

"It'll never happen, Mam," he had tried to reassure her. They both knew he was lying.

ഇന്ദ

Five Years Later

"Hello my girls!"

Grainne looked up at the squeals of joy and laughter from her twin daughters at the arrival of their father. Paddy knelt down on the grass, opened his arms and scooped them both up.

"Siobhan! Maureen! Come inside, now. Paddy, they'll muss up their dresses playing around like that," she scolded them, then sighed resignedly as she watched him playing with their girls.

She was instantly sorry for the scolding when she saw the way her husband and daughters' faces fell a bit as they were reprimanded for their display of affection. It was always a bit of a knife in her heart seeing Paddy with their girls. On the one hand, she was obviously thrilled that he loved them so, and they loved him. On the other hand, it reminded her so of how doting her father had once been with her at that age, memories she had spent a lifetime trying to forget.

"Come inside and wash up for your supper."

"Oh, come now; it's just a bit of play. Ye got to have a bit of fun every now and then, Grainne." Paddy bounded up the steps of the front porch and encircled her in his arms, forcing her to pause her task of folding the laundry.

"Says the one who doesn't have to do all the washing and mending when their clothes are ruined," she retorted, her tone still a bit more snappish than she had intended.

"And how are you, my wee man?" Paddy asked, turning his attention from his wife's usual peevish mood and finding distraction in their baby son, Connor. He lifted him from his bassinet, expertly cradling him.

"I just got him to stop fussing –" she protested, but Paddy was already dancing around the small porch, cooing at their son, who smiled and laughed as he saw his father's face.

She could not help but feel a tad resentful that Connor was never that happy with her. Paddy was a natural father, completely at ease with all their children. She had never really seemed to settle into motherhood, never really took to it. It was a sore point for her, particularly with her mother-in-law, whom it seemed was impossible to please when it came to raising her grandchildren.

Ever since she and Paddy had married, there had been a marked change in her relationship with Paddy's mother. Gone was the once affectionate woman who had helped show her how to survive life on Henrietta Street, replaced now with an overly critical woman who contradicted every decision Grainne made in raising her children.

First it had been the criticisms of how Grainne had moved her son out to the suburbs and planned to raise their children there. Next, it was the criticisms of how she designed the nursery and how she was still taking on some bookkeeping work even though she was married and pregnant. After the twins were born, it was the criticisms about how she fed and bathed the girls and changed their nappies. Everything she did was wrong, and Old Aoife O'Reilly could not help but point out every single detail. If Grainne had thought this was bad, though, things had gotten decidedly worse when it came to the twins' christening.

"Mam wanted me to let you know that Father Morris was after asking about the details for the twins' christening, and he just needs to know the date that we want to have it and then they can set all the plans in motion," Paddy had told her one day after he had come back from visiting his mother, gazing adoringly down at the girls while they had slept in their crib.

"Oh, that's alright," she had replied, with a tone of false cheeriness to hide the annoyance she had felt at her mother-in-law's interference once more. "I've taken care of everything with the vicar. We'll have the ceremony next Sunday after service."

Paddy had paused, stunned at this new revelation. "What?"

"I said that it's all taken care of."

"Ye mean you're going to have them baptised as Protestants?"

"Yes." She had looked at him like this should not have been surprising. "Of course."

"But…my whole family is Catholic. There's never been a Protestant in this family before."

"Except for me, and *my* family is Protestant, and my children will be too." Her tone had been firm, final.

"Your own mother was a Catholic," he had tried to point out after a moment's silence while the shock wore off.

"Well, it's what the Gallaghers would have wanted. They'll be christened at one o'clock on Sunday next. Your family is welcome to attend if they'll deign to darken the door."

Paddy had clucked his tongue in outrage but said nothing further. He never did when they argued.

"That woman'll ruin you, Paddy O'Reilly, you mark my words. She'll be the death of you," his mother had seethed to him later when he had told her about Grainne's plans.

From that moment on, there had never seemed to be a moment's peace between Grainne and her mother-in-law. Grainne went from being not good enough for her son because of her religion, to being too good for the likes of the O'Reillys because she wanted her and Paddy to be something more than what they had been before.

For the most part, Grainne tried to ignore her, but she would be lying if she said that it did not hurt a little every day. She had tried to console herself over the loss of someone she had once looked up to as a sort of mother figure when her own mother could not be bothered to parent her, by doing her best to focus on the life she and Paddy were building. There was something about being back in the outskirts of the city again, being surrounded by greenery and clean air again that made her dream of the possibilities in life.

The move had been good for Paddy too. She remembered when she had first taken him out here to see the house she wanted to raise their children in, and had watched as his face had lit up with wonder.

"What are you looking at?" she had asked him, observing how astonished he had seemed at the place.

"I'm just taking in all the green," he had exclaimed, acting like a child seeing an amusement park for the first time.

It was then that she truly realized that Paddy had never been outside of the tenements before. No matter how faint the memories of her childhood had become, she still remembered what it had been like to live outside of the city on her father's estate before she and her mother had gone to the convent. She had always known a life beyond the tenements had existed, but this was all new to her husband. Perhaps it was this knowledge that there was a world beyond the drudgery of Henrietta Street that began to make Grainne feel restless now, like she was not doing what she was supposed to be doing with her life or, at very least, like there was something more out there for her. So, when the opportunity came along, she had jumped at it.

"Paddy."

"Yes, love?" He was still dancing around the porch, their son tucked safely in his arms, a big smile on his face.

"I was talking to Mrs. Henry after church on Sunday, and she told me the most interesting thing."

"Oh…yes?" Paddy was still distracted, only half-listening to her. "Does Connor feel a bit warm to ye?"

"He felt a bit warm this morning, but his temperature was fine," she replied dismissively. "She mentioned how the college is holding some courses in the church basement three nights a week. Night classes, if you will."

"Who did?"

"Mrs. Henry. Are you listening to me?"

"Of course, I am. What kinds of courses, love?"

"Business courses: accounting…book-keeping, and the like. They're open to anyone who is looking to polish their skills, and you get a certificate at the end. I thought I might sign up for them."

In any other household, there would be a discussion between husband and wife about the wife taking any sort of classes or doing anything that was not directly related to the duties of being a wife and a mother. However, in the O'Reilly household, they both knew that Grainne was not asking for permission; she would do what she liked. She was just informing him of the decision once she had made it.

"It would mean finding someone to mind the children."

He stopped then and put Connor gently back in his bassinet. They both knew what she was saying. It was still frowned upon for a married woman to work after she got married, let Married women were still not technically allowed to work after they got married, let alone after she had children. And they both knew that these courses Grainne was taking were leading to exactly that: turning herself into a woman of substance with a job that was neither mother nor wife. She was not asking for his permission, but she was asking for his cooperation in her new plan for herself.

"Well, I'm sure we'll manage. The pub's doing well, and we've got enough extra that I'm sure we can afford someone to come in and help out a few days a week. If this is what ye want to do, then we'll find a way."

Grainne beamed up at him, pleased that no matter what she asked of him, he was always the one person in the world she could count on.

ꙮ

Starting that week, Grainne went to her courses three nights a week, working towards her certificate in accounting. Paddy had agreed that he could afford to bring on some part-time help in the pub, which would allow him to come home early those nights and get the children their tea and put them to bed, while Mrs. Henry from next door would come over for an hour or two and watch them until Grainne came home, and Paddy would return to the pub until closing. After six months of hard work, she finally obtained her certificate.

"I'm so proud of ye, love," Paddy said, kissing her on the cheek as she showed him her certificate. "Come now girls, aren't we proud of Mammy?"

"Love you, mam," Siobhan and Maureen chorused, dutifully coming over to kiss their mother on the cheek. Baby Connor gurgled happily in his father's arms, but Grainne knew his display of love was because he was only emulating his father's happiness, rather than any happiness he felt towards his mother.

Later that night, in bed, Grainne decided to tell her husband of the plan she had been working on since before she had begun her certificate, the plan she had to do something beyond running the household every day.

"Paddy?"

"Hmm?" She could tell that he was caught in that space somewhere between sleep and wakefulness.

"I've been thinking; I'd like to come and work with you in the pub."

"Mmhmm?" Sleep was still pulling at him and she was not sure that he was listening properly to her.

"I want to work with you in the pub. Well, not working *in* the pub, really, but doing the accounting, the office work…all the stuff you hate doing."

"Is that so?" He was starting to wake up now. He turned over, the mattress creaking beneath him, and sat up to look at her. "And what would we do with the girls? With Connor?"

He was not asking her to try and guilt her out of this proposition but because he was a good father who wanted to know how their children were going to be looked after if they were both working.

"I've been giving that a lot of thought," she proceeded cautiously. Even though he had always supported her in every decision she had ever made, she was not sure he was going to be happy by what she was going to say next.

"Well, now the pub is making a tidy profit for us, and we should have just enough to do it, I was thinking that we could send the girls to boarding school starting in the fall, and we could get someone in to look after Connor during the day while we are at work."

There was an unmistakeable deafening silence that descended upon the bedroom. A look came over Paddy's face, a dark look she had never seen before.

"Boarding school, Grainne? Really?" Paddy raised his voice at her, not seeming to care that the children were asleep in the room across the hall and could hear them if they raised their voices too loudly. In all the time she and Paddy had known one another, he had never raised his voice to her. It shocked her.

"It's a great school…" she began, even though his face got darker by the moment. "Villiers would be excellent for them, for their futures."

"A Protestant school?"

"Well, they *are* Protestants."

"A conversation that I wasn't a part of, by the way."

"No. I wasn't." Paddy's tone was sharp and biting. "You decided it for us, for them. You just told me what ye were doing without asking me about it first, like ye always do."

Grainne turned to look at him, shocked by his tone. This was not like him at all; this was not like the boy she had first met on the street outside of the tenement, like the man she had married. That man was always kind, always supportive. Sure, there were times when she knew she tried his patience or got on his last nerve, but he had never snapped at her like this before.

Paddy swiped a hand angrily across his face as he sat up in bed.

"I know ye've never really taken to mothering, Grainne, and I know ye want to be doing something more with your time, but sending the girls away to Limerick? Do ye really hate being a mother so much ye want to send the girls clear across the country?"

Her blood boiled at the suggestion that she did not love their daughters just because she wanted to send them to boarding school.

"That's not fair!" she seethed. "I love our daughters, and I want what's best for them."

"And what's best for them is to send them away?"

"I want them to have the best education, to have opportunities!"

"To have the kind of opportunities you would have had if your father hadn't thrown ye out, ye mean."

Grainne sat up straight then, the blood drained from her face, the blood pounding in her head as if she had been struck.

"Grainne…"

She got up from the bed and wrapped her dressing gown around her.

"Grainne, I didn't mean to say that."

"Yes, you did." Her voice was quiet, shocked. He had never thrown her father's abandonment in her face like that before.

"Grainne, I'm sorry. I'm just upset at the idea of sending the girls away. They're so young still. Maybe we can rethink this when they're a bit older, but for now, please say ye won't send them away.

She looked over at him, his eyes pleading.

"I haven't asked ye for much, Grainne. I agreed to get married in the Registry Office because ye didn't want to be married in the Catholic Church. I didn't stand in the way when ye baptised the children as Protestants, even though my own family threatened to disown us all. I encouraged you to keep working, even after we were married because I know it makes ye happy to work on the accounting. And I'm happy ye want to work in the pub and do the books for me. Frankly, it would mean the world to me if ye did that, because you're brilliant and amazing and would be an asset to the business. But I am asking ye now to not do this one thing, just for me."

Looking at those pleading eyes, Grainne felt herself wavering over her decision. Although everyone openly accused her of being stubborn – mostly because Grainne had neither the desire nor inclination to hide her determination – her husband could be every bit as determined as she was when he put his mind to it. He might be quieter about it, and he might choose his battles carefully, but when he wanted something, he was not afraid to go for it. However, once she had made up her mind to do something, there was no changing it. Paddy would just have to come around to the idea like he always did.

"This is what's best for them," she said firmly, hoping this would put an end to things.

Paddy's eyes darkened once more, and for the first time in her life, Grainne found herself afraid of what he might do. He rose from the bed, hastily pulled on his trousers, grabbed a shirt and headed downstairs. Stunned, Grainne followed him down to the front door where he had already pulled on his boots and coat. He took his hat from the hook by the front door and walked out, slamming it behind him, waking their son.

ജ്ര

Paddy did not return that night, or the one after that, nor the one after that. On the surface, Grainne acted like nothing was wrong; Paddy was just being contrary, but he would come around soon. Or, at least, this is what she told the girls when they asked her where their father was every day. Deep down though, it worried her that he had not sent word to let her know where he was at the very least. It wasn't like him at all to make her worry like this.

To make matters worse, Connor had been taking the separation from his father particularly hard and had been fussing all week, working himself up into a heated bother. She was nearly beside herself trying to calm him down.

"Shhhh, love. Come now, don't be like this." Grainne tried holding Connor and rocking him, but he was no sooner in her arms then he wanted down again. As soon as she put him down, he would start wailing again to be picked up.

"I know, I'm not the one you want," she commiserated with her crying son. They both wanted to see the one person who was not here right now. Grainne knew she could have called around for him, said what she needed to in order to have him come home, but she was not in the habit of losing an argument, so she had dug her heels in even more after he had stormed off.

"Come now, Connor, please just try to settle down," she pleaded with her infant son, picking him back up again as he held his chubby little arms out for her. She swiped his damp locks away from his forehead and noticed how warm he seemed.

"Lord, but you've worked yourself up good this time, haven't you?" She put the back of her hand to his forehead, worried that the warmth emanating from his skin might be more than just him being fussy. His skin did not yet feel feverish, but a feeling that something was not right began to sink into the pit of her stomach.

After a good forty-five minutes of dancing around the nursery and trying to shush him, Connor had cried himself into a fitful sleep. She put him gently back into his crib, hoping beyond hope not to wake him. She came downstairs and found the twins watching the telly.

"Come girls, it's time for bed."

The twins protested, but Grainne was exhausted and not in the mood for any more fussing from any of her children.

"I don't want to hear it," she snapped at them, and they looked at her sulkily. "Off to bed with the both of you."

"But Mammy, Da always warms us up a bit of milk before bed," Siobhan whined as her mother steered her and her sister towards their bedroom.

"Well, you can remind him of that when he comes home," Grainne snapped, ushering the twins into their beds and turning off the light.

If he comes home. The thought rushed into her mind before she could push it down.

Despite how exhausted she was, there was still this feeling that something was not quite right niggling at the back of her mind. She crossed the hall to look in on Connor again, something telling her that she should just make sure he was alright. She was not sure she would call it a mother's intuition; she did not think that was something she would ever possess, no matter how many children she had. Nevertheless, something told her to look in on her son.

She stood quietly in the doorway of the nursery across from the master bedroom, careful not to wake him if he was sleeping. She did not want to risk waking him if he was actually sleeping, as rest was be the best thing for him right now, but she also had to make sure he was fine before she would let herself relax enough to sleep. Peering into the crib, she noticed how his forehead was still damp, a sheen of sweat beading his skin. She carefully put the back of her hand to his forehead and noticed how much warmer he seemed, even though he had calmed down now.

She took out the thermometer she kept in one of the drawers nearby and picked him up. He began to fuss at being woken from his fitful sleep, but not like before. He was quieter now, his movements sluggish, like he was disorientated. She read the thermometer and began to panic. Grainne could not help but think how other mothers would have probably whisked their child off immediately to the doctor at the first sign that something was not right. Later, she would wish she had done the same and reacted sooner.

"Girls… girls!" She ran across to the twins' rooms, shaking them awake.

"We just got to sleep, Mammy," little Maureen complained, rubbing her eyes with the back of her hand.

"I know, love." She tried to keep her voice steady, tried not to worry them, but she knew that they still knew something was wrong.

"I need the two of you to put your clothes on," she told them firmly, helping them out of their beds and trying to locate some clothes for them.

"But it's bedtime, Mammy."

"I know, love, but we have to go for a bit of a ride tonight to the hospital." Grainne was not sure what else to tell them but the truth. Mrs. Henry and her husband from next door were away this week and she did not know anyone else who she could leave the girls with while she took Connor to the hospital. If Paddy were here…

But he's not. She firmly pushed down her fears for her son, and her anger at her husband, and got the girls into their clothes, picked up Connor and put him into his bassinet, and marched them all to the car. Thankfully, she had insisted Paddy teach her how to drive when they had gotten the car. Somehow, she had known that it would be useful in exactly a moment like this.

She settled the girls in the back of the car, with Siobhan in charge of holding her brother. Grainne put the car in drive and carefully drove down the street towards the hospital, her knuckles white on the steering wheel the whole way.

They arrived at the hospital in one piece, Dublin's streets mostly abandoned at this time of night. She carefully took her son from Siobhan's arms, herding the girls in front of her and walking inside.

"Can I get some help please?" she asked a passing nurse. "It's my son. He's really sick."

She was not sure if it was the desperate look in her eyes, but the nurse's tired posture seemed to soften a bit, and she directed her to an examination room.

"If you just wait in here, Mrs…?"

"O'Reilly."

"Mrs. O'Reilly. I'll have the doctor come and take a look when he can."

Grainne ushered the girls into the tiny exam room with her and Connor. Her son was still unnaturally warm, his whole body radiating heat like a furnace. She kept looking at him anxiously, not sure what to do. She did not like feeling so helpless.

Finally, close to an hour later, a beleaguered doctor stepped into the room.

"What have we got here?" No greeting, no smile.

"Something is wrong with my son. He's been warm all week, but he wasn't feverish until just tonight. He's had a bit of a dry cough, runny nose…and he's been fussing, and he's developed a rash in the last few hours."

"Ma'am, is your husband with you?"

Grainne was confused by the abrupt turn in the conversation. The doctor had not yet even looked at her son.

"Why do you need my husband here to tell you what's wrong with my son? I'm his mother."

"Of course," the doctor responded, his tone guarded, but also slightly bothered.

"Well?" she asked, pointing to Connor, who was now sleeping fitfully in his pram.

"It sounds like it could be a new tooth coming in, a cold…or a mother's worry." The last part he'd whispered under his breath as he fiddled with some papers, trying to make it look like he was writing something down, but Grainne could tell that he was only pretending. She quietly seethed at his patronization and belittling of her valid concerns for her son's safety.

"I know what a new tooth coming in looks like," she said through gritted teeth. "I have two daughters who have all their teeth." She nodded in the direction of the twins, who had fallen asleep in one of the chairs beside her. "I also know what the common cold looks like. This is not that."

The doctor sighed and made a move to leave the room, probably chalking this all up to some ridiculous made-up notion like hysteria.

"Well, I don't know what to tell you, ma'am. Take your son home and wait a day or so. I'm sure he'll be fine."

He walked out then, never once taking a look at her son. Grainne wanted to say she was surprised, but she was not. She was, however, extremely angry. Making sure the children were safe, she headed out into the corridor to give the doctor a piece of her mind, but he had disappeared.

"Excuse me?" she said to a nurse at the nurse's station. "I need to go and make a phone call to my husband."

"There's a telephone around the corner," the nurse replied, pointing in the general direction of the payphone without looking up.

"I need someone to watch my children, just for a few minutes."

"This is not a child-minding service, ma'am," the nurse sniped at her, still not looking up.

"I know…it will only be for a few minutes. I don't have anyone else to look after them." Grainne tried to hold her temper in place, but the hospital staff were really getting on her last nerve.

"Just be quick about it," the nurse said, finally getting up and going towards the examination room where the children were sleeping.

"Thank you," Grainne replied, her whole body wanting to collapse with relief at finally getting a bit of help, but she knew she had to find Paddy. If they would not take her seriously, perhaps they would listen to him.

When she got to the phone and began to pull out her coins, she realized she still had no idea where her husband was, exactly. She inserted some coins into the phone and told the operator to call her sister-in-law's house. She knew it was more likely that he had gone back to his mother's but no matter how many times Grainne had offered to have a telephone installed in her flat, her mother-in-law had always refused.

"If ye want to talk to me, ye can just come over and visit," she had snapped at her, trying to guilt them all about the fact that they did not come to visit nearly as much as she would have liked.

"Maureen, is Paddy with you?" she asked as soon as her sister-in-law picked up the phone.

After Paddy and Grainne had married, Maureen had gotten herself married and with a child by the one Dempsey brother who was, at least, not a criminal, even if he had not really made anything of himself yet. Wanting to distance himself from his family, he and Maureen had moved to a new set of flats not far from where Paddy and Grainne had once lived when they had been in The Liberties. While they still were not as close as they had been when they were children, away from her mother, Maureen had become almost sociable with Grainne again after awhile.

"It's important," she pressed when she had said nothing in response. "I'm at the hospital. Connor's taken ill." She swallowed hard, trying to stamp down the fear rising in her.

"He's over with Mam," Maureen finally replied. "He's been there all week."

Grainne cursed under her breath, knowing that this would be the case. It was the one place he knew she could not easily reach him.

"Well, can you tell your brother, then, that if he loves his son, he had better march himself down here to the hospital and speak to the doctor, because they won't talk to me. That, or he can forget ever coming home again." Grainne knew she sounded petty, but the whole ordeal of this week was catching up to her and she simply did not care what her sister-in-law thought of her. If all of the O'Reillys thought her haughty and imperious, then so be it.

"Give me some time to go over there and get him before ye go and leave him," Maureen said, her voice sounding serious.

"Thank you, Maureen."

She hung up the phone, relief beginning to wash over her.

ഋര

"I won't say I told ye so, but I knew if you moved away that something like this would happen," his mother practically crowed. She had been in a right jolly mood since her son had come home and told her about his argument with Grainne a week ago. He knew he should have gone straight home that first night – never should have left in the first place, really – but stubborn pride and a longing for home had kept him here. He knew his wife had never seen the tenements as home, but he felt comforted here, a sense of peace coming over him that he had not had since moving away.

The old flat he grew up in looked different to him now than it did before. He supposed that was what happened when you grew up and moved away. He noticed the wear and tear of the place more, the things he had ignored or just got used to when he had been a lad and did not know any better. Still, it was where he considered himself most at home, not that he would ever admit that to his mother. That would just give her even more to crow over.

"And I'd like to see *you* try and tell Grainne O'Reilly no when she puts her mind to something," he grumbled under his breath at his mother's comment. It still rankled with him that when he had finally put his foot down and told his wife "no" on one of the most important decisions of their lives that she had still dismissed him.

"Your too soft on her," his mother complained, seemingly picking up on his thoughts in the way only a mother can when they know their own child. "Ye let her run roughshod all over ye."

"No Mam, I just get out of her feckin' way when she's determined about something." But not this time. This time he *had* tried to stand in her way, for all the good it had done.

"That girl's always been too uppity for the likes of us. I told ye, ye shouldn't have married her. Marrying a girl like that who thinks she's better'n the rest o' us; what were ye thinkin'?"

"Leave off him, Mam," Maureen sniped as she came through the door to their old flat. He and his mother both looked up at her, surprised. It was very late at night and neither of them had been expecting her.

"What's brought you 'round at this hour?" he asked her, looking at the time on the small clock on the battered mantlepiece.

"Your wife," Maureen said simply.

Paddy rolled his eyes, but he was also just a little bit pleased that Grainne had been the first one to blink in their argument, the first to reach out and extend the olive branch.

"It's Connor. I think ye should really hurry over to the hospital. Grainne sounded…well, she sounded like I've never heard her before."

An icy feeling crept into the pit of Paddy's stomach and before his sister could say anything else, he had grabbed his coat from the peg by the door and had headed down to the car, speeding off to the hospital.

ꕥ

One Week Later

Grainne had been valid in her fears for her son. As it would turn out, baby Connor had contracted the measles and died in hospital only a couple of days later. What had seemed to be only mild symptoms the week leading to his death had belied the more serious condition that had gone unnoticed until it was too late.

Grainne and Paddy were beside themselves with grief, though both of them showing it in different ways. Paddy wore his heartbreak for all to see; it had always been easier for him to show his emotions. Grainne envied him that ability, especially now when she knew that everyone would be watching her every move, every tear that did not escape her bone-dry eyes even though she had just lost her only son.

They buried him next to her mother.

"Keep him safe, Mama," she whispered, touching her fingers to her lips and then to the headstone as they left the gravesite.

After that day, Grainne locked away every possible tear she could shed for him and buried the pain deep down inside of her where she would carry it for the rest of her life, like every other grief she had had up to this point. All those emotions inside her, swirling and festering; it was enough to make even the happiest person in the world the most cruel.

Connor's death marked their little family forever. Although Paddy had moved back, things had far from returned to normal. There was a distance between them now that had never existed before, a great emotional cavern that neither of them was sure how to bridge. Finally, one day, the distance was too much to bear.

"You blame me, don't you?" Paddy said suddenly to her, the two of them sitting in the front room together in silence. His voice had been barely a whisper. She had not been sure at first that she had even heard him, that she had not simply imagined it.

"What?" she asked, stunned.

"If I'd gotten there sooner…" his voice began to fill with emotion, and Grainne felt her chest constrict at seeing him in so much pain. There was only one person in the world she loved above any other, and she could not bear to see him hurt so.

"They said it wouldn't have mattered," she finally replied. "It was too late by the time we went to the hospital. It's a wonder you or I, or the girls didn't catch it."

Her chest constricted a bit more at the thought of how they might have lost the girls as well if they had caught the measles from their brother. She was not sure even she would have been able to be so stoic in the face of that.

"Is it wrong that sometimes I wish I had? That I wish I was up there with him now? Or that it had taken me instead?" his eyes looked upwards towards the heavens.

"I miss him too," she finally whispered.

Grainne felt a deep sadness wash over her. Moving closer to him on the settee, she pulled her husband close, partly to hold him while he sobbed against her chest, and partly just to feel him beneath her fingertips to reassure herself that he was still here with her. She could not imagine what she would ever do if she lost him too. That would surely break her heart beyond repair.

"Paddy?"

She felt his shoulders still a moment, listening to her, even though he had not said anything.

"Promise me something?"

"What is it, love?" He brought his tear-streaked face up to look at her.

"Promise me you'll never leave me." Fear still gripped her chest at the thought of it.

"I promise, love. I'll never leave you ever again."

Chapter Six

Although neither of them had said it out loud, from that day forward, Paddy and Grainne were united in all decisions. Even though they knew their argument had not been the cause of their son's death, neither of them wanted to tempt fate.

Grainne got her way in the end, and the twins were sent to boarding school in the autumn. However, even Grainne did not have the heart to send them all the way to Limerick, and so they were sent to St. Columba's College in Sandyford, just south of the city. They were able to come home on weekends and holidays, which pleased Paddy, and that pleased Grainne. Now, with the daily responsibilities of parenting absent from her routine, Grainne had time to focus once more on turning herself into something she had wanted to be since she was little older than her own daughters: a woman of substance.

Dublin
1967

While it would not be for another decade that the restrictive "marriage bar" would be lifted in Ireland, bringing about a much-desired step forward in women's rights in the country, Grainne O'Reilly was not the type of woman to hang about and wait for some official to tell her what she could and could not do. She was a leader, not a follower, and she had many a big plan to usher in a new era for *O'Reillys*.

"We could really make something of it, you know," she said to Paddy one night in bed.

"Make something of what?" he asked sleepily, drifting in that space between sleep and wakefulness.

"*O'Reilly's* of course!" she replied excitedly, as if it should have been obvious to him from the start. Grainne's mind moved so quickly from thought to thought that she sometimes still forgot to take into account that she did not always relay half the information swirling around in her brain to the person she was speaking to, and so they were often left in the dark on some of the more salient details.

"We are making a go of it." Paddy's voice indicated he was beginning to nod off again.

"No, I mean it's time to take things to the next stage."

"And what stage would that be?" Paddy turned around now and sat up in bed, the mattress shifting and creaking beneath him, knowing he was not going to be getting any sleep until his wife had said her piece.

"Opening a second pub. Turning it into a franchise. I was talking to Frank McNally about it, and he says that now would be the right time, financially, for us to expand. The pub's been doing well for over a decade now and shows no sign of slowing down, and we can really capitalize on that and begin our own franchise."

"Expansion? Franchise?" Paddy might be awake now, but his brain still felt muddled with all these new terms his wife was telling him about. She was right that the pub had become very successful, especially of late. In fact, he had just been thinking the other day that he was going to have to hire on some more staff, but expansion? He had never considered that.

"And where would we expand to?"

"Oh, I've already found a site. We just need to put in an offer."

Paddy knew what this meant. Since Grainne did not technically own the pub, she needed his signature and approval on any and all ideas she had for it, especially this idea of expansion. He could have been angry with her for going ahead and putting everything in motion without having spoken to him about it until now, but he had become so accustomed to his wife's way of doing things that he simply did not want to argue with her about it.

"Oh, and we really need to bring women into the pub," she continued. "They make up half of this country, and that's a whole half of the population that we could be making money from that we just aren't. I mean it, Paddy. We could really make this work."

His brow drew down as he mulled over her idea, seeing only one flaw in her plan. "I know ye mean it, love, but there's not a man in the whole of Ireland who's going to take ye seriously about it. Women just don't frequent the pub."

"Because men won't allow them in," Grainne snapped. "The pub is as integral to the fabric of Irish society as the family, and which church you attend," she stated matter-of-factly. "If men would get their heads out of their arses, then they'd realize that women working a long day want a drink in the pub at the end of the day just as much as any man. And why should women be excluded? We're allowed to drink just as much as we want at home, so why not in a pub?"

Paddy could see no reasonable objection to the case she laid before him. He secretly admired the way she did that:

building up an argument he found difficult to poke holes in. It was infuriating for sure, but it was also something he loved about her.

"Just think about it: if we open up *O'Reilly's* to include women, think of the number of patrons we'd have over the competition."

"Unless ye count the men who'd stop coming because we're letting women in," he pointed out, though he did not disagree with her plan. He was not against women being in his pub; he just did not think they would want to come.

"It's the 1960's for Christ's sake," she exclaimed. "If they don't want women in the pub, then we don't want their custom."

Paddy could see she was set on her plan and would go ahead with it whether or not he agreed with her. She was not asking for his permission; only letting him know that this was how she was going to be moving forward, and he could jump on board with the idea, or not.

"Well, looks like we'll be needing a contractor then," he stated.

Grainne gave him a curious look.

"Well, if we're going to have women, *and* we want to keep the customers we have, I was thinking we should build a snug by the bar. That way the women can enjoy their drinks in private, if they like, and no one need cause a fuss about it."

"And their pints," Grainne stated.

"Now don't be going and pushing things," Paddy warned her. "Ye know well that pubs have the right to refuse to serve women pints. Ye can't be going and changing the whole world in a day, much as I'm sure ye'd like to think ye can."

He gave her a small smile to soften the words.

She narrowed her eyes at him but seemed to sense that this was one of the few arguments she might not win. At least, not yet, anyways

"And if they don't want to be hidden away out of sight?" she asked, prepared to get her back up over his other idea about the snug, but he could that she was coming around to it.

"One step at a time, love. We'll start with the snug and see how things go from there."

ꟿ

Things took off from there. Frank McNally, the lawyer Grainne had hired to handle their legal affairs, had been instrumental in helping her to acquire the future site of the second *O'Reilly's.*

"Frank says that we just need to find ourselves some investors to help pay for the expansion, and then we can turn this all into a proper franchise."

"And where does Frank hope that we're going to find these investors?" Paddy asked, looking up at the abandoned pub they had just acquired. The place was going to need a whole lot of fixing up if they hoped to be able to have it up and running by the end of the year – as was Grainne's intention – and he knew that was not going to come cheap. But Paddy knew this was something very important to her, and she would stop at nothing to make it happen. Although he might be the public face of *O'Reilly's*, there were few who were in doubt that it was Grainne who was actually running the business, and had been doing so for years. In fact, he had to credit his wife with most of their success over the last decade. She had set herself to the task of not just keeping the books, but also elevating the status of their family in Dublin society, making the right kinds of connections with the right kinds of people at just the right time. She was very good at it: the hob-knobbing, almost like she had been born to it. It made him proud to see how much she had accomplished for them all in such a short amount of time. While he might not know where she planned to find these investors she was hoping for, he had no doubt she would find them in the end.

"I've a few ideas," she replied absent-mindedly; he could see that her mind was already racing with idea of how to turn the current run-down site in front of them into the start of a most profitable venture for them.

"I'm sure ye do, love," he smiled at her. All that was left now was to leave her to it.

ꕥ

Six Months Later

"Keep your eyes closed," Grainne instructed, a smile on her face. "No peeking!"

"I'm not! I promise."

She waved her hand in front of his blindfolded eyes, making sure. When she was satisfied he was telling the truth, she came around behind him to untie the blindfold.

"Ok, one…two…three!" She lifted the blindfold from his eyes and came around to see his reaction.

She knew before she looked into his eyes that he had not liked it. He would not say so, of course, but Paddy had never had a talent for keeping his expressions off his face. Not with her, anyways. She had known deep down he would not get her vision for *O'Reilly's*, that he would not be able to see the future of the business in the same way she could.

"Well now…" he waved his hand expansively at the restaurant around them, taking it all in.

"Of course, you hate it," she snapped at him. She did not want to be like this right now. She wanted him to be in this with her, to want this with her as much as she did. They had agreed after Connor that they would be together in all things, but that had mostly meant that he had just let her do whatever she thought best. He was not a true partner in this venture, and that made her sad. She hated that he just could not see everything they could do together if he would only just dream a bit bigger.

"I didn't say I hated it." His tone was calm, trying to be conciliatory.

"You didn't have to. With you, Paddy O'Reilly, what you don't say is always more important than what you *do* say." She looked at him, knowing her eyes were sad and tired, and frustrated.

"It's fine, love…I just…"

"Well, if it's just *fine* then…"

"Oh, come on now, Grainne. Ye know I didn't mean it like that."

She stood there with her hands across her chest, her posture defensive. She had not expected him to exactly gush over the design of the place, but she had been hoping for a bit more than *fine.*

"It's just…It's not really what I expected is all. It's so…"

"So what?"

"So different from the original pub, is all. It's just a different…what's the word ye used…aesthetic. It's a different aesthetic." He looked at her, his eyes pleading with her not to let them argue about this. "The other place is just more *me*, I guess."

"Well, if you have a pub that's more you, then this place is more me," she remarked. "What would be so wrong with that? Am I not an O'Reilly just the same as you are?"

"Of course, ye are, love."

"So, what's so wrong about it, about me, then? What is it you hate about us both?"

Paddy's nostrils flared a bit and his posture tensed. She knew she had hit a nerve with him, not just because she was picking a fight after they had promised each other they would never fight again, but also at the implication she was making.

"Maybe you think your mother was right after all and you married the wrong person."

"Don't say that." Paddy crossed the short distance between them and put his hands on her upper arms, turning her to face him. He was so close to her she could smell his aftershave, and the hint of cigar smoke underneath it. He knew she hated it when he smoked, but he still managed to sneak one in behind her back every now and then.

"I am not your father, Grainne. I am not going to wake up one morning and find fault in my wife and girls, and suddenly put them aside for my own ambition. I know the person that I married, Grainne. Can you say the same about yourself?"

She looked up at him, her bottom lip trembling ever so slightly, and she could have cursed it for making her seem weak to herself.

"What is so wrong with me wanting to make a better life for us all?" she asked, deflecting from his question.

He sighed. "There's nothing wrong with that, love."

"Then why can't you see that this is how we do that? This is how we will make that better future for ourselves."

"It's not you or your vision that I doubt, Grainne." He was looking straight into her steel-grey eyes now. "In fact, I don't doubt any of it. It just all took me by surprise, is all."

"Sometimes, Paddy O'Reilly, I wish you would dream just a bit bigger."

"I leave the dreaming of our future to you, my love," he said, and pulling her in closer to him. "I have everything I need right here in the present."

ꙮ

"It's God awful, that's what it is," his mother said the next day, looking around the place and taking it all in.

"Mam…" Paddy's tone was resigned more than chiding. He could not blame her for her opinion. After all, it was only yesterday that he had taken in all the fancy new décor Grainne had put in that was so unlike the original *O'Reilly's* in Temple Bar. Gone was any trace of personality or sense of home. It was all clean lines and simple palettes, no mismatch of designs from a family pub that grown up over generations, with each one trying to put their mark on it. This

"Well, it is!" she exclaimed, barely bothering to keep her voice down. A few patrons who had come for the grand opening of the new and improved *O'Reilly's* looked over in their general direction, curious about the storm cloud of tension that was about to break over their table.

"Apparently the decor will do very well with the Americans." He shrugged. What did he know of these things? If Grainne said it would work, then he was sure it was. He had complete faith in his wife's idea for the business, after all, she had not let them down yet.

"The Americans! And what do you or Grainne know about America? Sure, and ye've never even set foot outside of Dublin before."

"I told ye before, Mam: Grainne wants to turn *O'Reilly's* into a franchise. She says there could be many an *O'Reilly's* across Ireland, Britain, and even American soon enough. Maybe even further afield," he parroted his wife's words. He knew them by heart now, Grainne had been saying them so often lately.

"Grainne's been talking to…"

"Grainne, Grainne, Grainne! It's not even her name, O'Reilly. That's *your* name above the door."

Paddy gave his mother a dark look. Things had never particularly smoothed over between his mother and his wife, not even after Connor's funeral. If there had been one good thing that might have come out of that heart-breaking tragedy, Paddy would have wished for two of the most important women in his life to find some way to co-exist peacefully, but it seemed that the Fates would deny him even that.

"She's my wife, Mam. She's a much right to the name as you."

His mother harrumphed and stewed silently a moment at the implication that she was in any way similar to her upstart daughter-in-law.

"You're already thinking of expanding further even though ye've only just gone and opened a second pub?" His sister's tone was full of surprise. He had not really discussed Grainne's plans with either her or his mother, knowing full well what they would think of them. If his mother was not complaining about how Grainne was neglecting her duties as wife and mother, she would have complained about Grainne's ambition, that she was expanding too rapidly. He had that same fear, that perhaps they were taking on too much with a second pub, let alone expanding further across the country, but he also had absolute faith in his wife's business sense. He had no idea where she had inherited it from; certainly not her own mother, but her sharp mind for figures and a keen sense for giving customers what they wanted had meant that they had had opening day figures that had far exceeded expectations.

"Alright here?" Grainne asked, coming over to the table and sitting down next to him.

"Wonderful, love." He gave her his best encouraging smile, and it thrilled him to see a happy pink blush rise in her cheeks. He knew she was loving every minute of this opening and he wanted all the happiness in the world for her on her special day. "Mam was just admiring the work ye've done with the place, weren't ye, Mam?"

His mother glowered at him but had been raised too politely to ever say to Grainne's face how much she might hate the design of the pub. "Yes, what a…lovely place ye have here."

She looked around the place like she was trying to find something to compliment but, finding none, she decided to switch topics.

"And how are the twins? I'd have hoped to see them today."

"Yes, well I should get back to the guests and check with the kitchen; just make sure that everything is still running smoothly."

Grainne hurried from the table, and it saddened him to watch her go, knowing that it was because he had done the one thing she had asked him not to: invite his family on her big day. He knew the pressure she felt from them, but he could not help hoping that if his mother just saw all the effort Grainne was making that maybe, just maybe, one day the two of them could find some common ground again. He was sorry that, despite his best efforts, he seemed to be letting his wife down at every turn.

ꙮ

Malahide
1970

"Are ye sure ye couldn't find a bigger house?"

"Oh stop!"

He playfully dodged her attempt to take a swat at him. He moved around behind her, encircling her in his arms and resting his chin on his shoulder, observing the massive pale red-brick mansion in front of them.

"*That* is a big house," he reiterated.

"Isn't it beautiful?"

Paddy lifted his chin to watch her gazing up at the house and saw the gleam in his wife's eyes at the splendour in front of them. In his opinion, it was not so much what Paddy thought of the place, but whether it would make Grainne happy. It was all he had ever wanted: to make her happy. He had often felt lately like he was coming up short on that mission, but maybe this house would be just the thing that would make her stop and realize that she could be happy now. She had spent so much of her life waiting for the next terrible thing to happen that she had never really learned to live in the present and enjoy what she had. Maybe this new home would be the thing that finally made her happy again. He hoped it was true, even if somewhere in the back of his mind he knew the idea was a fantasy.

"And how are we going to pay for it?" he asked her, his voice taking on a pensive tone.

"We have a loan from the bank," Grainne replied, as if it were obvious.

"But isn't it a bit much to be buying such a large place now when we're looking to expand and open another pub?" Paddy looked at her seriously.

"I swear, Paddy O'Reilly, that you will be a millionaire and you'll still worry that you can't pay for anything," she teased him. "You don't live in the tenement anymore; you don't have to worry. We have plenty of money. Besides, you have to spend money to make money, and this is exactly the kind of house that tells the world that we have money."

A short silence fell between them as they stood gazing up at their new home.

"What are we going to fill it with?" he asked, wondrously, changing topics. "It's bigger than a whole row of houses!"

"Oh, don't you worry Paddy O'Reilly; I have big plans for this place," she said excitedly, heading towards the front door.

"I'm sure ye do, love," he chuckled, following her inside. "I'm sure ye do."

ꕥ

"Mrs. O'Reilly?"

"Yes, what is it?" Grainne did not look up as her assistant poked her head around her office door. Along with the whole new look and feel of *O'Reilly's*, Grainne had also decided to make this her headquarters of sorts and had built a little office area for herself into the back of the building, a place where she could go every day to get her work done, and escape home when she wanted to.

"There's a gentleman here to see you, Mrs. O'Reilly."

She looked up then, confused. She had not been expecting to see anyone today.

"Send him in," she commanded after a moment's pause to ensure she was presentable.

"Julian Lynch, Mrs. O'Reilly. It's nice to meet you."

A distinguished man of about fifty with a thick New York accent, dressed in an impeccable suit, entered the room and offered to shake her hand.

"Lynch? You wouldn't be over here trying to find long-lost relatives, would you?" She had asked it more for something to say than out of any real curiosity but was surprised to hear that she was right.

"Actually, that's exactly what I'm in Ireland for."

It should not have come as a surprise, really. Many Americans had been back to the homeland of late, so to say. It was almost as if a whole national wave of nostalgia had hit the country and they had decided to come and play the tourist in what had once been their home.

"However, I didn't come back here to talk about long-lost relatives," he started, taking a seat opposite her desk, comfortably commanding the room from her. "I wanted to talk to you about your pub here. It's astounding what you've done with it."

"Thank you. My husband and I put a lot of work into it." She had unmistakeably emphasised the "I" in her response.

"Well, if the two of you ever have plans to take this place and turn it into a chain, you can call me any time." He handed her his business card.

She took it from his hand and ran her fingers idly over the fancy embossing.

"Thank you, Mr. Lynch. I hope you're serious about that offer, because if you are, I have a feeling that you and I are going to have a lot to discuss."

ꟹꟹ

"I thought you'd be happy about this." Grainne's face took on a petulant look. "This is what we've always wanted, what we've always dreamed of."

"This is what *you've* always wanted," Paddy corrected her. His tone was not harsh, nor angry, just matter of fact.

"If you had your way, we'd be back in the tenement." She sighed and put down her book on the beside table.

"Well, I can think of worse things." Paddy's tone had been low, but still loud enough for her to hear.

"And is that what you truly would have wanted for us? For our girls? To grow up poor and continue to be poor the rest of our lives? Never knowing from day-to-day whether there'd be food to put on the table for your supper or if you'd have to go to be hungry? Don't you want things to be easier for them? For us all?" She was stung that he still could not see how everything she had done so far, everything she was currently doing was for the betterment of their family. Even though he did not say it outright, sometimes she felt that he thought she was only doing this for herself, which was wildly unfair.

"Of course, I do. Ye know I do, Grainne." Paddy gave her a pained look, hurt by the accusation that he would rather their family were starving than living in a mansion. "But I also don't want them growing up thinking that money is the only important thing like…"

The unspoken words hung there a moment before she snapped, "Like me? You don't want them to grow up to be like me. Vain and spoiled, just like your mother and sister think of me. That's what you're saying isn't, Paddy O'Reilly?"

"Ah, come on now, love. Of course, that's not what I think of ye." He leaned over in the bed put his index finger under her chin, tilting it up ever so slightly so she had to look him in the eye. She loved looking into those eyes of the clearest blue she had ever seen, like the colour of the sky on the sunniest of days. "I think you're smart, and brave, and the most beautiful girl I've ever seen in the whole wide world."

He gave her one of those charming smiles then, the type he knew would always make her feel like she was the most special person in his world. It worked, of course, and she dipped her head so he would not see the small smile tugging at the corners of her mouth.

"And what would you know of the world, Paddy O'Reilly?" she asked, punching him playfully on the arm. "You've never been farther than Sandyford."

"I don't need to see the world to know you're the prettiest thing in it."

"How can you know that if you've nothing else to compare me to?"

"I just do," he replied simply. "Ever since the day I met you, you've been the only thing in the world that I have ever wanted. And if taking *O'Reilly's* to America is what ye want to do, then I'll be standing right there beside ye to make it happen, for I've no doubt that one day you will be one of the most successful businesswomen this country has ever seen."

Grainne smiled at the vision of that and thought that, perhaps now, she was finally starting to become the person she had always wanted to be.

Epilogue

Dublin
Forty Years Later

Grainne took a deep breath to steady herself before she entered the hospital room. She hated hospitals; always had, especially after losing her son nearly fifty years ago now. It was difficult not to wonder what he would be like now, a fully-grown adult with a family of his own, and maybe even young grandchildren. She could have been a great-grandmother by now. The thought both shocked and pleased her.

Time was a curious thing. It passed without you really realizing it. She had grown old before she had known it, her mind still somehow impossibly believing she was still the same young woman as she was when she had first married Paddy and moved out of the tenements. She supposed that that was when she truly had begun to feel like she had been coming into her own, when she was becoming the person she had always wanted to be. Despite the decades that had passed and the success she had amassed, a small part of her still felt that she was still looking for that woman, that she was still coming into her own. A part of her wondered if she would ever truly find her.

Grainne shrugged away the thought as she entered the room, putting on her best brave face. It was no easy feat; it nearly broke her heart every time she walked in here. After all she had endured in her life, she thought perhaps that seeing Paddy lying there in his hospital bed, looking thinner and frailer by the day had been the hardest yet. He had said he had not wanted to come here to die, that he had wanted to be at home, but ever wanting to please his wife, he had complied with her wishes when she had insisted that he be admitted to the hospital. She knew it would not prolong his life, that no miracle cure would be found to save him in time; she did not even have much faith in the hospital staff to look after him properly. It was merely a placebo to help her remain calm in the face of the one thing her mind could not contemplate. But seeing him in here every day now, she had to live with the regret she felt that she could not just let him have this one last wish, that she had just had to make him come in here so she could feel some semblance of being at peace with the worst thing she could imagine: him dying and leaving her here all alone.

He was dozing when she entered the room, not fully asleep. He could not sleep properly in the hospital, he had told her. It made him look even more weary with every passing day.

"Hello, my love." His voice was whispered and cracked, dry from disuse and weariness. She came over to his side, bringing a glass of water with a straw to his lips so he could drink.

"That's better," he sighed, settling himself back into the pillows. Grainne reached behind him and began to fluff them, even though she knew they did not need it. Paddy gently took her hands, forcing her to stop her fussing.

"And how are you today?" she forced herself to ask, trying to keep her tone even and steady, more for her sake than his.

"Oh, ye know; can't complain."

She smiled at him and a little laugh escaped. Here he was with every reason in the world to complain, to be angry, or frustrated, or whatever; and here he was with a smile on his face and a not a word of complaint. He was simply marvelous.

"Aoife came 'round to visit earlier."

Grainne tried not to keep her expression neutral. "Oh really? That was nice of her."

"Ye can't fool me, Grainne O'Reilly. Never could," Paddy smirked at her.

"I don't know what you mean," she remarked, playing coy with him.

"Do me one favour? Try not to be so hard on Aoife."

Grainne made a guttural noise in the back of her throat, which she tried to cover with a polite cough. In the way of Irish families, two of their grandchildren, Connor and Aoife, had been named for others in the family. Aoife, of course, had been named for Paddy's mother. And how she lived up to the name!

"She's an O'Reilly through and through, that one. She's just like your mother: stubborn, wilful; and she's just like you in that she can't get out of her own way to see what's best for her." She reached down to smooth the hospital bed covers that did not need smoothing.

"She sounds like a certain other O'Reilly I know," Paddy remarked quietly, but loud enough that he knew she would hear.

She threw him a dark look. "She is capable of so much more but she's content to waste it all away while she drifts through life. She should settle down with that Danny and start a family before he gets other ideas."

Paddy made a face at the mention of their youngest granddaughter's boyfriend, which she pointedly ignored. They were on opposite ends over Danny's suitability as Aoife's boyfriend, with Paddy firmly against him.

"I'm not so sure I'm in any rush to see those two get married," he said. "Besides, there's nothing wrong with her being happy as she is right now. There's no hurry for her to settle down. Let her live life a little."

"Well, fine then. If she wants to throw away all that potential, then I'll stay out of it."

He raised his brows, clearly not believing a word she said.

"I mean it!" she exclaimed, momentarily annoyed with him. "I'll leave her be and not meddle, but I won't let her influence Connor to waste his life away."

Their grandson, Connor had, naturally, been named for the son they had lost. Grainne had considered it the best gift she ever received the day that their daughter, Siobhan, told them she had wanted to name her son in honour of her late brother.

"As our only grandson, it's his duty to be the head of the company. He's already put it off for so long by joining the military. I won't have Aoife wasting all of his potential on grand ideas along with her own." Grainne was firm on this.

"Some would consider it an honour to have a grandchild in service to their country, ye know." His tone indicated that he was such a person.

"Well, bloody foolish is what I think of it," she snapped. "He could have been shot any number of times over there in the desert, so far from home. I've not had a proper night's sleep since he joined up, and neither has his mother. He's like to give us both a heart attack if he carries on like that."

"He'll be perfectly fine," he reassured her, putting his hand over hers. "God has other plans for that one. Besides, Caitlin knows far more about running the company than he does. She's always shown a knack for the business. Ye should make more of an effort to spend more time with her, really show her how it's all run."

When she was born, Paddy had said it was a good thing that Caitlin had not been named for anyone else in the family. As she had grown older, and it had become more and more obvious that Connor had little interest in the family business, despite Grainne's best efforts to force him into it, it was Caitlin who had stepped in as her grandmother's natural successor. She was no Grainne O'Reilly, but she still had some of her grandmother's knack for business, and Paddy had said it would be a good thing that when it was time for Caitlin to make her own mark on the company, that she would have a name of her own and not have to live up to anyone else's legacy.

"Caitlin's too…" Grainne struggled to find the right words. There was no doubting that of her two granddaughters, Caitlin was certainly her favourite, but that favouritism paled in comparison to the love she felt towards her grandson who, in many ways, Grainne had felt was a sort of second chance at raising a son. "She's too eager to please, too much of a follower."

"She just needs a little guidance to come into her own," Paddy reassured her, placing his hands on hers. She was surprised to feel how papery-thin his skin had become.

Grainne rolled her eyes at him.

"Be kind to them, Grainne, for your own sake, if for no one else's," he cautioned her, his tone serious now. "I worry that if you push too hard, you'll push them all away for good, especially Connor and Aoife. And that won't just break your heart; it'll break theirs too." He reached up a hand to stroke the side of her face. "Let them see you the same way I do, just once. Let them in. You might be surprised to find they're more like you than any of you realize."

She scoffed at him.

"They may have different dreams than you, but that doesn't mean that they are any less ambitious. Look at Aoife. She's never been content to stay in one place, to do only one thing, much like you were when you were her age."

"I think your medication is playing with your mind," she retorted, but he continued on.

"Aoife, Connor and Caitlin all have your resiliency; they just show it in different ways. None of them lets life keep them down. They'll all thrive in whatever they choose to do, but I worry that if you stand in their way, they'll push you aside, and that will hurt you more than you'll ever admit to them."

Grainne looked away, knowing that her eyes would betray her and show him that she knew what he said was true. She admired all of her grandchildren in her own way; not that she would ever let them know that, especially Aoife. It would give that wilful nature of hers even more reason to be headstrong and determined.

"There's only one thing in this world that could break my hear, Paddy O'Reilly," she replied, suddenly serious. She had not meant to show him how much she cared, but hearing all this talk of the future with their grandchildren, a future they both knew he would not be a part of, had let the emotions of the past few weeks since he had revealed his diagnosis creep up on her.

"Hey now," he said, his voice soft and concerned as he noticed a couple of tears slip down her cheek. She had not cried in front of him in over fifty years, and she hated that she was breaking down now at the end. "What's got ye upset?"

"I'm upset, Paddy O'Reilly, because you broke your promise to me. You said you wouldn't be the first to leave."

"I know. I'm sorry, my love." He gave her a pained expression, and all she wanted to do was lean over and sob into his chest, rail at him for leaving her and how unfair it all was, but they both knew she would not do that. She had spent an entire lifetime building up walls around her. Just because Paddy may be able to see through those walls did not mean that she opened them up for him.

She cleared her throat, trying to regain her composure. "I have to leave you now. I have that interview today."

She had been asked to do an interview about the success of *O'Reilly's,* chronicling its rise and the massive international success it had become. When asked to do the interview, she could have done the polite thing and included her husband in it, made it a joint effort. But Grainne was not like other people, and while it might have originally been only her husband's name above the door on the first *O'Reilly's,* Grainne felt that in the last forty years, she had more than earned the family name that was stamped across the front of hundreds of pubs across the world. She was the one who had taken a small pub in Temple Bar and turned it into an international chain. She was the one who had turned this into more than just a family-owned pub like so many others. She was the one who had made her family, and herself, a success.

"Go on then, love. Show them all what you're made of."

ꕥ

"Grainne, may I call you Grainne?" the young woman conducting the interview asked as she pulled out her mobile to begin recording.

Grainne nodded at her.

"You have the most incredible story," the young woman stated. "You rose above your upbringing in the tenements, and your mother's death, and then the death of your adopted parents…"

"Stop, stop," Grainne snapped peevishly at the reminders of the ghosts of her past. "If this is the story you are planning to tell, then let's just stop here."

It was a bold move, she knew. However, after the last few weeks she had had, and having had a glimpse of the future without the one person in the world that she had always been able to rely on earlier that day, Grainne was feeling more than a little annoyed.

"I don't want to be one of those stories about a poor girl who achieves great success in spite of some great tragedy. That is not why I began this company, and that is not how I would like to be remembered."

"How *would* you like to be remembered, Grainne? What is the story *you* would tell about yourself?"

She did not hesitate with her answer.

"I'd tell the story of a woman who got everything she deserved through hard work, grit, and more than a little determination. That's what makes me the woman I am, and that's what makes me a success story worthy of your attention."

Did you like *Grainne O'Reilly*? Leave a review!

Grainne O'Reilly can be found on the review site of your choice.

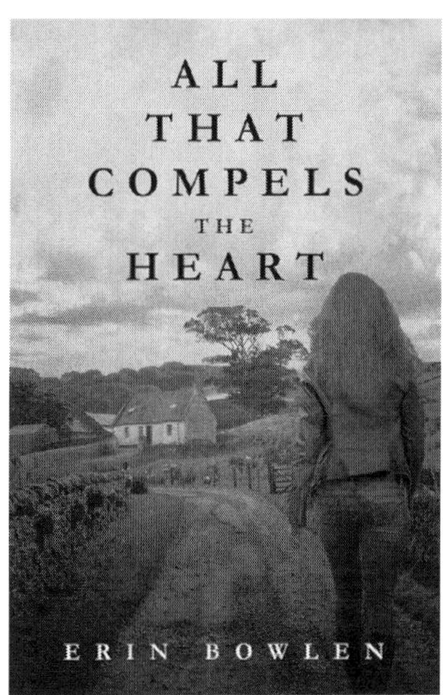

She's always seeking the next adventure. But is the passion she yearns for right on her doorstep?

Dublin, Ireland. Aoife O'Reilly's life is almost the way she wants it. Apart from her dysfunctional family, she's grateful for a steady job and a bright future to embrace. But when she's made redundant from her job and her beloved grandfather dies in the same month, she impulsively moves to an idyllic village to sort herself out.

Settling in the quaint little town so very different from the big city, she's quickly frustrated by developing feelings for her handsome-but-engaged neighbor. And just as both he and the charming atmosphere begin to grow on her, the opportunity of a lifetime arrives.

Can Aoife discover who… and where she's meant to be?

All That Compels the Heart is the engrossing first book in the Aoife O'Reilly new adult women's fiction series. If you like deeply drawn characters, lyrical sagas, and slow-burn chemistry, then you'll love Erin Bowlen's moving journey.

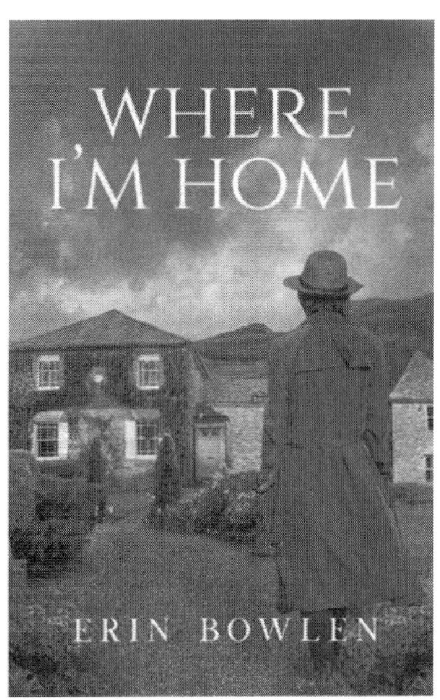

It's not often that you get a second chance at love.

New York City, USA. Three years ago, Aoife O'Reilly made a life-changing decision to follow her dreams. Now, between a successful new career and starting a new family with her partner, Colin Lee, Aoife is seemingly at peace with that choice. But when a phone call comes to let her know someone close to her has passed away, Aoife finds herself rushing back to Ireland.

Ballyclara, Ireland. It wasn't easy for Michael to start over again after Aoife, but he got through it, in no small part due to the love and kindness shown to him by Ailish. Finally, able to see himself settling down into the life he's always wanted, Michael dares to dream of a life for the two of them. But the peaceful bliss he and Ailish have managed to find is upended with Aoife's return to Ballyclara.

Confronted by the ghosts they thought they'd put behind them, Michael and Aoife must re-evaluate the choices they've made. Are they better off in their new lives? Or is their love one worth fighting for?

Acknowledgements

I'd like to take the opportunity here to acknowledge, first and foremost, the kinds of conditions the former tenants of the Henrietta Street tenements (and other tenements just like them throughout the rest of Dublin) lived in. Today, as I sit in my apartment, writing this during the midst of a global pandemic, I could complain about the state of things. However, writing Grainne and Paddy's story, researching the squalor of the tenements from the mid-1800's to the mid-1900's, I'm immensely grateful for everything in my life. With this novella, I tried to balance both sides of tenement life: both the hardship of living without running water, without indoor plumbing, and of having no proper place to cook meals or a proper place to sleep; with the sense of community and shared experience that those who grew up in tenements very like the ones described here have expressed in memoirs and personal stories that I've read and researched.

For information on Dublin's tenement life, I'd like to draw your attention to 14 Henrietta Street, a social history museum which strives to bring awareness about life on Henrietta Street from its Georgian beginnings, up to its final days as a tenement in the 1970's. You can find out more information about their conservation efforts for the 14 Henrietta Street building, as well as tours and other information on their website. I would also draw your attention to a particularly helpful documentary about life in Dublin's tenements, appropriately called "The Tenements," which was a four-part series about Dublin's tenements, but had a particular focus on Henrietta Street.

If life in the tenements was harsh and unforgiving, life in the Magdalen laundries were their own special hell. There are no accounts of the lives of the women who found themselves in these asylums that I've read that didn't break my heart, and I must have read dozens of these accounts while doing research for this novella. Numerous newspaper and journal articles exist with accounts of life in the Magdalene laundries. There are also several films and books (both fiction and non-fiction). In particular, I found the Martin Sixsmith book, "The Lost Child of Philomena Lee," helpful. Although Philomena's story doesn't take place at the same asylum as that mentioned in this novella, it still provides an insight into the harrowing existence of the women who found themselves sent to these laundries.

After researching the Magdalene laundries and the tenements, I thought that things could only get better from there (and they did, eventually). However, it was clear in reading the work of Catriona Clear; Elizabeth Kiely and Maire Leane; and Ashling Sheehan, Elaine Berkery, and Maria Lichrou, that working women between the 1950's and the 1970's was one of sexism, discrimination (both social discrimination and gender discrimination), unequal pay, and so much more. Although there are many accounts of working women's lives during this time period, the work of these women mentioned above were particularly helpful for me in understanding the kinds of challenges Grainne would have faced as a woman who went against the traditional role the society of her time would have expected of her.

Researching this novella has taught me so much about Irish women: their resiliency, their bravery, their compassion, and their determination for a better life, a better society, and a better world. I think that it's important to honour what these women have fought for to get Irish women's rights to where they are now, and I hope this novella helps inspire you to go beyond the story and dig deeper into the fascinating history of women in Ireland.

On a personal note, I would like to thank Jeremy McLean from Points of Sail Publishing and Victoria Cooper from Victoria Cooper Art for their work on the formatting and cover art for this novella. I'd also like to thank in particular, Sarah, Janet, Bill, and Charlotte for always demanding more from me with this series. And to all the fans of the Aoife O'Reilly series: your support, as ever, means the world to me.

About the Author

Erin Bowlen was born and raised in New Brunswick, Canada. Growing up, she was influenced by her family's artistic roots in the art of storytelling, which fostered a deep love for literature at a young age.

Erin began her writing career during her postgraduate studies at the University of New Brunswick. Finding herself at the crossroads between being too much of a storyteller to be a "proper" academic (and afraid she might be too much of an academic to be a storyteller), she took the advice of a friend to participate in a 30-day writing competition. At the end of the month she was surprised that she not only met her word count goal, but had several novel ideas to explore.

In 2018, she published her first novel, *All That Compels the Heart*, the first book in the Aoife O'Reilly series.

Where I'm Home is her second novel.

Erin currently lives in New Brunswick.

Printed in Great Britain
by Amazon

11110116R00072